THE TUXEDO™

Based on a story by Phil Hay &
Matt Manfredi and Michael Wilson

Screenplay by Michael Wilson
and Michael Leeson

Adapted by Ellen Weiss

DREAMWORKS®

Published by Price Stern Sloan,
a division of Penguin Putnam Books for Young Readers
345 Hudson Street, New York, NY 10014
TM & © 2002 DreamWorks
Text by Ellen Weiss

ISBN 0-8431-4966-3

1 3 5 7 9 10 8 6 4 2

Printed in the United States of America

The forest was deep green and peaceful, dappled by the sunlight that filtered in through the treetops. A light wind rustled the leaves, and the birds chirped busily to each other.

A perfect, crystal-clear drop of water trembled on a young leaf, finally sliding off its edge and plummeting downward to join the sparkling stream that ran below it.

A little farther downstream, a doe and her fawn stood drinking at the stream's edge. Wading deeper into the water, they both casually answered the call of nature, adding their own somewhat yellower liquid to the rushing water.

The stream was moving faster now, getting more swollen, becoming brown and murky. Soon it was swallowed up by a roaring cave mouth. Rushing underground, the water thundered its way through the earth's dark passages until it was finally sucked up into a huge, rusting pipe. Inside the pipe, all the larger junk—gravel, sand, and sediment—smashed into metal screens and was filtered out.

And at the other end of the pipe, the barely filtered water spurted from steel nozzles to fill up thousands of plastic liter bottles that marched along in single file below it.

The water had arrived at the Banning Bottling Plant.

As the bottles shuttled along a conveyor belt, blue caps were popped onto them by machines, and finally, a mechanical hand slapped a label onto each one. The label said BANNING SPRINGS, PURITY OF ESSENCE. The labels were graced by an idyllic illustration that showed two deer by a crystal-clear stream.

At the end of the line, a machine shrink-wrapped the bottles, and another packed the plastic pods into shipping boxes. Uniformed workers loaded the Banning Water boxes onto wooden pallets.

On this particular day, a group of business-men was being led on a tour of the factory. A uniformed worker stood near the loading dock, watching them inspect the facilities. Then he ambled toward a stairwell door. In the relative quiet of the stairwell, he pressed a cell phone to his ear.

"It's Wallace," he said hoarsely into the phone. "Operation Big Drip is cresting level two. I need Chalmers and I need him now...Don't put me on hold!"

Annoyed and angry, he shook the phone, but it was no help. The tinny strains of "America the Beautiful" issued from the receiver. He pressed the phone to his ear again.

Abruptly, a clear plastic bag was thrust over his head from behind by a pair of thick hands. A cord was yanked tightly around his neck, bagging his head and the cell phone together.

Wallace flailed helplessly as he was lifted off the floor. Meanwhile, water began filling the bag, rising past his chin, his mouth, his nose, his eyes. He had very little time to try to figure out what was happening, for he was already breathing in the liquid. His hair undulated in the water like seaweed.

When he had ceased struggling, a rubber hose was yanked out of the bag from behind. Water spilled out as the bag was removed from Wallace's head, and then his limp body tumbled down the stairs.

A tall beast of a man turned and hunched up

the stairs. On his back was a pressurized water tank, the tank that had forced the water into the plastic bag over Wallace's head.

The man spoke into a walkie-talkie. "Cleanup to sector D stairwell," he said. "Somebody spilled something."

Outside the Strick Art Gallery, Jimmy Tong was getting his face right. He thought he had it. Radiant with intelligence. Handsome without being intimidating. And the smile was good. It conveyed endearing shyness. He was wearing a T-shirt, chinos, a knee-length cotton coat, and sneakers. "Hi," he said. "My name is Jimmy Tong, and I was wondering if there's anything I could say that would convince you to come and have lunch with me."

"You're so cute," said the man's voice beside him. Mitch, a man with the spirit of the Caribbean in him, grinned at his friend Jimmy.

"You got me nervous again," Jimmy said.

Mitch shook his head. "Man, she's just a salesgirl," he told Jimmy.

"To you," Jimmy replied. "But to me—I dreamed of her before I ever saw her."

"That's good. Tell her that," suggested Mitch.

"'Hi. I'm Jimmy Tong. I dream of you before I see you.' Is that what I said?" he asked.

"Just go with the lunch thing," said Mitch.

Jimmy straightened his coat and marched into the gallery.

Inside, the place was full of serious modern paintings and unfriendly looking metal sculpture. Jimmy squinted at a painting, doing his best to appear as if he was considering buying something. He was observed by the owner, a sharp-looking young man in an expensive suit.

Across the gallery, a pretty young woman, fashionably dressed, was talking to wealthy couple about a painting. They were finishing up.

Jimmy's heart pounded as the young woman gave the couple her card. He winced at his distorted reflection in a polished metal sculpture and straightened his lapel, silently rehearsing what he was going to say. Waiting until the couple was gone, he finally approached her.

"Hi," he said.

She looked at him, and his mind went blank. To cover his confusion, he turned to examine a painting. It was a weird, dark, abstract piece.

"Pretty colors," he said lamely.

"Will you excuse me a moment?" she said. She crossed to her desk to make some notes. Jimmy continued to take deep breaths to calm down as he gathered the courage to saunter toward her desk. He glanced at her, but she held up an "I'll be right with you" finger.

Jimmy smiled a little too broadly and nodded. Then he continued to peer at the painting.

The gallery owner appeared at his shoulder and gazed at the painting alongside Jimmy. "The use of negative space," he said, "the way the central image is a sculptural, post-impressionistic element...it impacts you on a visceral level, doesn't it?"

"The frame is nice," tried Jimmy.

The owner bent down to speak confidentially into Jimmy's ear. "Just between us guys," he murmured, "you don't come around here for the art, do you?"

"Who would?" said Jimmy softly, involuntarily glancing at the girl.

"Let me, as the owner of the gallery, give you a little piece of friendly advice. Waste no more time, go over, and ask Jennifer out."

"You think?" said Jimmy hopefully.

"Yes, because then she can say no, and we can all get on with our lives," snapped the owner.

"Thanks for the advice." Jimmy paused and briefly regarded a particularly grotesque sculpture. "Your mother pose for that?" he asked.

"Good-bye," said the owner.

Mitch was waiting outside as Jimmy came churning out.

"I don't want to talk about it," said Jimmy.

They crossed the street, heading for the line of taxicabs that was parked at the curb in front of a hotel, waiting for fares.

"Did she turn you down?" Mitch asked.

"No."

"Did you ask her?"

"No."

"Jimmy, come on, go back in there, get properly rejected, be a man," Mitch exhorted him.

"Mitch—back off," said Jimmy.

They had reached the line of cabs, and Jimmy opened the door of his.

"I'm getting a hot dog, you want one?" asked Mitch.

"I'm not hungry," replied Jimmy.

Mitch left, and Jimmy sat in the driver's seat of his cab, his brain buzzing. He picked up a dog-eared book from the seat beside him: *Amassing Wealth for Dummies*. He put it down.

Idly, he took one last glance across the street at the gallery. And, like a divine sign, Jennifer emerged.

Jimmy went into a quick rehearsal under his breath. "Hi. I'm Jimmy Tong. Is there anything I could say to convince you to have lunch with me?" Then he took a deep breath and threw open his door.

Bam! Out of nowhere, a bicycle messenger hit the open door like a bomb. In a split second, the tattooed, pierced courier had somersaulted over the door and hit the street.

Jimmy scrambled out of the cab to help him up. Out of the corner of his eye, he saw that Jennifer had paused to watch.

"I'm sorry. Are you hurt?" Jimmy asked the messenger.

The messenger sprang to his feet, already in full attack mode. He was like a mad dog, sending a barrage of kicks and punches at Jimmy.

Jimmy was scared witless. "We're two adults!" he cried, ducking a kick.

On the sidewalk, a small crowd of passersby had gathered to watch. Among them was a well-dressed, self-assured-looking woman with dark brown hair and pale skin. She looked coolly interested in the proceedings.

Jimmy had no time to notice any of this. He shot himself in and out of car windows, desperately evading the messenger's assault. "Use your words!" he admonished the fellow.

Jimmy was fast, but the messenger caught

him in a headlock. And on top of all this, Jennifer was walking away.

"There's no reason for violence!" Jimmy yelled at his assailant.

Now Mitch reappeared, munching on his hot dog. Quickly taking in the scene, he ran to help Jimmy, pulling the messenger off by his eyebrow ring. "Let go of him, I say!" he shouted.

"I'll bust you up, too!" the messenger threatened.

"Don't mess with me!" Mitch warned, tossing the bike to the messenger. "I killed bigger snakes than you with my bare hands and a little stick!" He pulled a yellow pencil from behind his ear and used it to jab at the messenger, who finally gave up and rode away, his front wheel wobbling.

"Yeah, go get a tattoo of a chicken!" Jimmy called after him as he slid out from under a car.

Mitch shook his head. "I thought all you Chinese people know karate," he said to Jimmy.

Jimmy was upset. "My mother sent me to tap dancing!" he protested. "Not every Chinese person is Bruce Lee."

Mitch brushed him off. "Calm yourself, Jimmy," he said.

"I'm cool, Mitch," Jimmy said. "It's just not my day." He climbed into his cab.

Once inside, he took a deep, calming breath. *Okay, just relax*, he told himself.

"Think you can get me to 700 Fleming Street?" said a woman's voice behind him.

Jimmy jumped. In the backseat was the dark-haired woman who had stood watching the messenger incident.

"Sure," said Jimmy. "No problem."

"You're Jimmy Tong?" she asked him.

"That's me. Who are you?" He started the engine and pulled out.

The cab moved fast but smoothly through heavy traffic. "The name's Steena," she said. "I'm a little confused, because in Chicago you were Johnny Bing, before that Jeffrey Dong, Jackie Tang, Jerry Ting, Joey Bong—you're running out of bell sounds."

Jimmy was tense now. "You a metro cop?" he asked.

"I know a few," she replied. "How come you drive so fast?"

"More fares," he answered.

"That's why you had your license suspended nine times for speeding?"

Jimmy took a look into his rearview mirror. The woman was pale because she wore no makeup at all.

"But no accidents," Jimmy pointed out.

"Until now," said Steena, looking ahead.

Something in her expression made him glance forward just in time to see a dog walker with ten small dogs in the crosswalk. He jammed on the brakes. The dog walker glared, and the dogs all yapped ferociously as they herded across the street.

"Remember where I'm going?" Steena asked dryly. She took a makeup bag from her purse.

"700 Fleming."

"Get me there before I finish putting on my makeup, and I'll double the meter," she said.

"Are you serious?" he asked.

"Do I look like I have a sense of humor?" she replied dryly.

She opened a lipstick tube and Jimmy punched the accelerator.

The taxi surged forward, veering into an opening in traffic. Its tires screeched. Jimmy drove like a madman, maneuvering through the traffic at top speed. He was either very good—or very lucky.

Steena touched the lipstick to the corner of her mouth as the cab tilted into a turn. "A little to the left, please," she said as the lipstick glided across her bottom lip.

The taxi careened around the tattooed bike

messenger, causing the man's second crash of the day. Oh, well.

Steena's lipstick glided back over her top lip.

Jimmy checked her progress in the rearview mirror. "Looking good," he said.

"I'd watch the road if I were you," Steena said.

Up ahead, the street was blocked by a large garbage truck. To the right was a large gate on which was written the words, IRON ROOSTER POULTRY CO. TEL. 555-WING.

Jimmy quickly punched in the numbers on his cell phone. "I got a load of ducks!" he shouted into the phone. "Open up!"

The gate opened. Jimmy veered into the entrance, blasted through a narrow passage inside, scattering feathers all the way, and pulled the cab back out onto the street beyond the garbage truck.

In the back of the cab, Steena sharpened an eyeliner pencil, looking only slightly impressed by his driving. "I have eyeliner and mascara left. You have five blocks," she said.

Jimmy accelerated around a corner, only to find the street clogged with traffic. Steena smiled to herself, looking pleased by this new obstacle. "Don't tell me you're slowing down," she said.

They heard the sound of sirens. Jimmy looked

into the side-view mirror and saw two fire trucks coming up from behind. One of them barreled past, and Jimmy's cab jumped in line right behind it.

The firemen on the back of the truck waved him away, and Jimmy waved back happily.

They waved harder. The sirens wailed.

"Sorry, did you say something?" Jimmy mouthed at them, pointing at his ears.

As the taxi streaked through the traffic sandwiched between the fire trucks, Jimmy checked Steena in the rearview mirror. Her hand was now shaking as she applied her mascara.

"It's the next street," said Steena.

"You're too helpful," he replied.

"To the right," Steena added.

There was only one problem: a one-way street sign, pointing to the left. Steena, regaining her composure, started to apply mascara to her other eye. She had the upper hand again. "Guess you'll have to go around the—"

Jimmy made a hard right into oncoming traffic. He stomped the brake pedal, threw the cab into a 180-degree skid while shifting into reverse, and backed up the one-way street.

The cab slalomed backward through traffic, until Steena's head jerked backward as the cab stopped: 700 Fleming.

"We're here," Jimmy announced. "And I beat you by an eyelash." He hit the meter. It read $9.35.

Steena leaned forward and handed him a twenty. "You lived up to your reputation," she said. "The job is yours."

"I have a job," he said. "A good one."

"How much do you make at this good job?"

"Four seventy-five a week," he told her. "Plus tips."

"And you wouldn't be any happier making two thousand a week? Plus room and board?" she asked with a shrug.

"When do I show up?" he said quickly.

She handed him a business card. "Tomorrow morning, seven o'clock," she said. "Drive carefully."

She got out, slamming the door. Jimmy looked at the card. It read: CLARK DEVLIN, 1007 RIVERWAY ROAD, HEATHSTEAD, L.I.

2

The next morning, Jimmy was in Mitch's cab, still holding the card eagerly. They were traveling down a country road lined by hedges. Jimmy was dressed casually, as usual, in jeans and his khaki coat.

"My plan is," Jimmy was saying, "I work for this Clark Devlin a couple years, save up some money, go back to Shanghai, and open a coffee shop."

"Coffee?" said Mitch, surprised.

"Chinese people are sick of tea," Jimmy said.

Mitch drove on for a while before he said, "I've heard about these rich bored women. They hire you and then before you know it, they turn you into some kind of slave."

Jimmy stared at him looking worried.

"Money drives people crazy," Mitch explained.

"That's true," Jimmy agreed.

"I've had rich guys in my cab, always in a hurry to go no place," Mitch said.

"And they only drink water out of bottles," Jimmy added. "I don't mean the big bottles, I mean the little ones. Turn here."

Mitch turned the cab into a wide driveway that wound its way uphill. At the top was a spectacular mansion.

The two men were totally awestruck, but neither one would ever admit it.

"Who'd want to live in that?" said Jimmy.

"I wonder what it would cost to heat a place like that," Mitch commented.

"I'm gonna miss our apartment," said Jimmy, hoping his friend wouldn't miss him too much.

They had finally arrived at the huge front door and Jimmy climbed out of the cab. Cracking his gum, he turned and waved good-bye to Mitch.

Mitch leaned over so he could see his friend. "Be cool, Jimmy," he said. "Call me."

After Mitch pulled away, Jimmy walked up the steps to the carved wooden doors, looking for the doorbell. As if by magic, the door opened.

There stood a butler in a pastel shirt, slacks, and a bow tie. "Follow me, please, Mr. Tong," he said.

Stepping inside, Jimmy looked around the

grand entry. He immediately bumped into a very expensive-looking sculpture, almost knocking it off its base. Luckily, the butler caught it before it hit the floor.

"You should glue that down," Jimmy said sheepishly.

Wordlessly, the butler showed him into a well-appointed office. Inside, Steena was sitting at a desk, writing.

Jimmy stood in the doorway, still chewing his gum. The butler disappeared.

"You put your face on without me," Jimmy said to her.

Steena didn't crack a smile. She stood up and approached Jimmy, a leather folio under her arm. In her outstretched hand was a sheet of paper. "Lose the gum," she said.

He put his wad of gum onto the paper, whereupon she balled it up and gave it to him. Then she gestured toward a chair. Jimmy sat.

"Also the mildew on the chin," she said.

"My soul patch?" said Jimmy, horrified.

Ignoring him, Steena dropped the leather-bound sheaf of papers on his lap. "House rules," she said. "Memorize them. Especially number one."

Jimmy opened the cover and began reading. "'Never talk directly to Mr. Devlin,'" he quoted.

"If you have questions, you'll find the answers in there," said Steena.

"You like working for this Devlin guy?" he asked her.

"I don't work for him."

Steena shut her attaché case and strode out. Jimmy just sat there, confused.

In a moment the butler reappeared, startling him. "I'll show you to your room. Try not to destroy anything on the way," he said.

Jimmy's new room wasn't home, but it wasn't bad. There was a radio, which he immediately tuned to a jazz station. Then he threw his clothing over a chair and went into the bathroom to shower and shave.

He emerged rubbing his clean chin, not liking the feel of it. The music abruptly stopped and was replaced by static. Then there was a beep, and the butler's voice came through the speakers. "Mr. Devlin will be leaving in ten minutes," it said. "Bring the car around."

Jimmy opened the shades and looked out at the garage courtyard. Below him was a gleaming limousine.

Next he opened a closet, and found it to be filled with gray uniforms: shirts, caps, and shoes.

"Don't forget the cap," said the butler's voice.

Ten minutes later, Jimmy had the limousine idling in front of the mansion.

Dressed in a gray uniform and cap, he struggled to knot the tie evenly. Finally he gave up and tucked the long end inside his shirt.

The rear passenger door opened and closed with a precise *thunk*. Jimmy looked in the rearview mirror, tilting it to get a better look at his employer, Clark Devlin. He was a sophisticated and good-looking man, impeccably dressed in a well-tailored suit.

"I'm not a professional driver," the man said, "but I believe the reflective device into which you're peering was designed to allow the monitoring of rearward traffic, not passengers."

About to respond, Jimmy remembered Rule One: Never talk directly to Mr. Devlin. He readjusted the mirror, shifted into drive, and stepped on the accelerator.

The limo hurtled down the country roads and then entered the expressway, threading through the traffic.

In the back, Devlin watched a stock market report on TV and talked quietly on a cell phone. "A conundrum solved prematurely becomes a morass," Jimmy heard him say. "We don't want that, do we...?I'll call you when I have something definitive." He shut off the phone and pushed in the antenna. "He cultivates impatience in hopes someone will mistake it for intelligence," he said. "What do I do? Descend to the level of my superiors?"

"I know," said Jimmy. "Just because you work for some guy doesn't mean he knows more than you—sorry."

Uh-oh. Jimmy realized he had just broken Rule One by saying something really stupid.

Suddenly, brake lights flared ahead. Jimmy checked his right mirror, then veered across three lanes and took an off-ramp.

"You took the Balsam Road exit," said Devlin, not looking up.

"Better to go surface streets. Traffic stacks up this time of—oops. Sorry, again."

"Steena gave you a copy of the rules?" asked Devlin.

Jimmy started to answer but caught himself in time. He nodded.

"I hate those rules," Devlin said.

Jimmy hadn't expected this. He checked the rearview mirror.

"By the way," Devlin said, "if you take Grant Boulevard, all the lights are timed."

"Thanks for the tip," said Jimmy.

Time went on. Jimmy did his job, wore his uniform, and collected his very generous pay. Three weeks later, he found himself standing in a some sort of fancy establishment, much like a jewelry shop, waiting for his employer to finish transacting some business.

Jimmy looked around at the elegant glass cases. Inside them were display trays filled with insects of all colors and sizes. Other cases in the store held arcane entomological instruments.

Jimmy watched Devlin, who was deep in conversation with a salesgirl. More than words seemed to be passing between them.

"My contact in Guatemala can find what you're looking for, I'm sure," said the salesgirl.

"In the meantime," Devlin replied, "I'll take this *Dystiscus marginalis*."

He held up an iridescent blue insect impaled

on a pin, gazing at it as her blue eyes gazed from the other side. Devlin's focus shifted to her eyes.

"Extraordinary color," he said.

The salesgirl looked steadily at him. "Is your phone number on file?" she asked.

"I never can remember it exactly."

"Some things need to be totally right to work at all," she replied.

"I could go home and call you with it," said Devlin. "Or, if you're free tonight, I'm having a small gathering. Shall I send a car?"

"I drive myself."

"Admirable." He pushed the pin through one of his cards and handed it to her. "Eight o'clock? Did I mention it's a fund-raiser for the natural history museum?"

"I'll chip in," she said.

"Don't wear anything too stunning," he said, "or nobody will pay attention to the chamber orchestra."

She laughed and lowered her eyes. Jimmy knew that Devlin had successfully charmed her.

Outside on the street, Jimmy carried the purchases as Devlin walked to the limo.

"How did you learn to be so smooth?" Jimmy asked him.

"You have great instincts. I see that when you drive. That girl in the art gallery is not beyond you, you know," Devlin answered.

Jimmy was shocked. "You know about her, too?"

"Wherever we're going, you manage to drive by there. All you need is some polish."

"You can't polish a brick," said Jimmy. "I'll never be a Clark Devlin."

"I'm going to let you in on a little secret, Jimmy. I've got a few good moves and some expensive suits. Other than that I'm just the same as you."

"How about the couple hundred million dollars?" Jimmy asked.

"It adds a glow, I admit. But I really believe ninety percent of it is the clothes."

"And the other ten percent?"

"The suit gets you the date," Devlin said. "The ten percent wins her heart."

"Mr. Devlin," said Jimmy, "I have a big favor to ask."

"What?"

"Can I stop wearing the hat?"

Devlin took the cap off Jimmy's head. "Better," he said.

"Thank you," said Jimmy, greatly relieved.

While balancing the boxes, Jimmy opened the car door for Devlin.

"Thank you," said Devlin. He climbed into the car as Jimmy stowed the packages in the trunk.

While Jimmy was busy in the back, Clark pulled out his cell phone and punched in a speed-dial number. "Steena," he said, "this driver you found, I think he's a keeper. He's going to be needing a proper suit...Expedite that for me, will you...? Lovely talking to you, too."

The driver door opened and Jimmy got in. Clark smiled at him. "Home, James," he said cheerfully.

4

Diedrich Banning's ship was elegantly furnished. The furniture, simple yet perfect in design, was made from beautiful and rare woods.

Banning sat in the ship's hold with a scientist named Dr. Simms, who was scanning information on the screen of a laptop.

"Why did you choose Lundeen?" Simms asked.

"He questioned my growth projection," Banning replied. "And I don't like his hair."

A platform elevator descended. On it was Banning's accountant, Lundeen. He was a middle-aged man with a Beatles-style haircut. He was accompanied by Kells, the large man who had wielded the killer pressurized water tank at the bottling plant.

"Mr. Banning, I'm honored to be invited aboard," said Lundeen.

Banning rose to greet him as he stepped off

the elevator. "Have you met Dr. Simms from research and development?" he asked Lundeen.

"Haven't had the pleasure."

"Well, you've had it now," said Banning. "Word filtered down to me that you don't share my optimism about our company's future." Banning poured some water from a pitcher into a glass, which he slid in front of Lundeen. "Drink?" he said.

"Thank you," said Lundeen. He took a sip. "No," he continued, "actually, I just felt that to meet your projections, every person on earth would have to drink only Banning Springs water."

"Thank you for clearing that up," said Banning.

"I mean, we are talking about a specialty product—" Lundeen went on.

"Specialty product?" Banning said. "I'm sure you're familiar with Maslowe's Hierarchy of Needs. What's at the base? Air and water. Water, Mr. Lundeen, comprises sixty percent of your body."

Lundeen was not looking that well. Sweat beads had begun forming on his forehead. Simms leaned forward, interested in his physical state.

Lundeen took another sip of his water.

"Don't you find it incredible," Banning

continued, "that two hydrogen atoms and an oxygen atom can create something so beautiful, so useful, so essential? You drink it, you wash with it. Immerse yourself in it and you defy gravity. Water is a miracle. You think I'm silly."

"Not at all," said Lundeen, sweating profusely now. He took another long swallow.

"Feeling thirsty?" Simms inquired.

Banning smiled at Lundeen. "You're helping me out by being a guinea pig for a new product," he told his accountant.

"Oh...Oh!" What a brilliant idea!" Lundeen said, being a good sport. "Water that makes you thirsty. What's in it? Salt?"

"There's no elegance to salt," Banning said dismissively.

"Bacteria." Simms grinned. "Once ingested, their DNA instructs your cells' cytoplasm to spill electrolytes into the bloodstream, causing dehydration." He was clearly in love with his own idea.

"Huh!" Lundeen said, still trying to look enthusiastic. His skin was now beginning to pucker.

"It's virulent but a bit quick," said Simms.

"As we speak," Banning added, "every one of your organs is shriveling."

"Wow..." said Lundeen. And that was the last

word Mr. Lundeen ever said, for he was turning to dust. His skin swiftly wrinkled and contracted, his eyeballs deflated, and his hands became bones covered in yellow parchment.

"You're becoming as dry as your limited imagination," Banning said, patting Lundeen's shoulder. Lundeen's body crumbled under his touch.

"It's so beautiful, I almost feel like crying," sniffed Simms.

Banning was not so sentimental. "Kells? Get the dustmuncher," he said.

Kells produced a dustmuncher and began vacuuming up Lundeen.

Back at the mansion, Devlin walked from his room, dressed in a tuxedo. His tie was untied.

Jimmy happened to be passing by. "I didn't hear tonight is black tie," he said.

"It's not," said Devlin. "But you never know what might happen."

Jimmy pointed to Devlin's bow tie, reminding him that it was untied. Devlin nodded and turned away for just a moment. When he turned back to face Jimmy, the tie was perfectly tied.

Jimmy wasn't sure what he'd just seen, it had happened so fast.

Devlin smiled, and they continued on their separate ways.

The party was magical. In the Great Room, an audience listened raptly to the orchestra that was playing Haydn's *Serenade*. But Devlin was not among them. He was out on the terrace, dancing with the insect salesgirl, who looked stunning in a sequined dress. Devlin's tuxedo shimmered with a phosphorescent glow.

Standing inside, Jimmy watched Devlin dance. He tried to copy his boss's grace, using a gate as a stand-in dance partner.

Outside, the butler approached Devlin and the girl, carrying a tray that held two glasses. As he neared them, however, he stumbled, nearly dropping the tray. Devlin, in a flash, stretched backwards, caught the tray, and quickly righted the butler. Not a drop of champagne had been spilled.

The butler took the tray back from Devlin, nodded a curt thank you, and walked away. Jimmy gazed at the scene, blinking. What had he just seen? It seemed almost supernormal.

A beautiful woman in a red dress approached Jimmy, a champagne glass in her hand.

"You had to escape, too," she said to him.

"Too much hot air in there," he replied.

She laughed. He was not sure why.

"It's a full moon," she said.

Jimmy's shyness began to grip him, as always, but then he recalled Devlin's move with the salesgirl back in the shop.

"That is lovely," he said. "I could look at it all day."

She was clearly enchanted. He couldn't believe it had worked for him.

"I'm Angelica," she said.

"James," he replied.

"I haven't seen you at one of these before. You're on the museum council?"

"No. I work with Clark Devlin."

"Then you must know your way around," she smiled. "Shall we wander?"

"Admirable," said Jimmy.

She put her arm through his and they started down a nearby path.

But they had not gotten far, when the walkie-talkie crackled with static. "Jimmy, bring the car around," said the butler's voice from the speaker.

Jimmy clamped his hand over it.

"—and Mr. Devlin wants you to replace the Forest Glen air freshener with Springtime in Taos," continued the butler, his voice muffled now by Jimmy's hand.

The beautiful woman looked at Jimmy. "You're Devlin's driver?" she said.

Jimmy shrugged and then nodded.

"I thought you were an actual person," she said. "I'm really slipping. Sayonara." She walked away.

"Sayonara," said Jimmy sadly.

6

The next day, Jimmy was carrying some dry cleaning up to Devlin's room when he passed by a window and saw Devlin outside, standing beside an ornate birdbath. Devlin was photographing the surface of the water. Jimmy just shook his head. He thought to himself, *Rich people are weird.*

He paused at the doorway to Devlin's study, where the butler was fussily polishing a collection of eggs. This was just one of several unusual collections the boss had. Jimmy inspected a display of fragile objects.

"Why is Mr. Devlin taking pictures of the birdbath?" Jimmy asked the butler.

"He has wide-ranging interests. Two months ago he was obsessed with monosexual deep sea-fish, before that Haitian voodoo rituals. Last Christmas it was all about practical applications of string theory." He sighed deeply. "The rich," he said. "Too much time to dabble."

"When does he work?" Jimmy asked.

The butler shrugged. Jimmy returned the shrug and turned to leave, but as he did, the dry cleaning bag snagged on the display case and knocked over a number of fragile pieces.

The butler motioned to Jimmy to just leave.

▰

Clark Devlin's room was as impressive as the man himself. Jimmy entered it, carrying the dry cleaning into an extensive walk-in closet. It had built-in bureaus, shoe racks, and glass-fronted wardrobes filled with suits, shirts, and pants arranged in spectrums. At the end of the closet, hanging alone in a glass case, was the tuxedo Devlin had worn the night before. Jimmy started hanging the cleaning on matching brass hangers.

But his attention was drawn to the tux. It looked so perfect, so potent. It looked as if it had absorbed Devlin's charisma.

Jimmy moved toward it, noticing as he got closer the incredible stitching on the tux, the nearly unseen details that elevated the suit to the realm of the wondrous.

He reached for the brass doors and pulled. They did not open. He gave them a tug, and then a slightly harder tug. It was almost as if the tux

were denying him access. Just one more firm
yank—

"There *is* one rule—" said Devlin's voice behind
him.

Jimmy whipped around, caught. He started to
say something, but Devlin wanted no explanation.

"Never. Touch. My tuxedo," he said.

"I didn't," said Jimmy.

"Don't," said Devlin.

Jimmy bundled up the dry-cleaning hangers
and bags and started to leave in a hurry.

"Jimmy," said Devlin, "would you like to join
me for dinner tonight? We'll go out."

◼▶

That night, in the car on the way to dinner,
Devlin sat in the back doodling on a piece of
paper. He was drawing a sketch of a spidery insect.

"Let's turn in here," he told Jimmy. "Get a
bite."

Jimmy signaled, slowed, and turned. In the
back, Devlin folded the piece of paper into a small
square.

"All right!" said Jimmy, delighted at Devlin's
choice. "B.K."

Jimmy and Devlin rolled down their windows
in front of the Burger King order speaker.

"What'll you have?" said Devlin. "I'm buying."
He handed Jimmy some bills.

"Double cheeseburger, chili fries, large Coke," Jimmy said into the speaker.

"Anything else?" said the disembodied girl's voice.

Devlin leaned toward the speaker and said, "Pizza, crisp crust."

"Your order's ready," said the girl.

Jimmy examined Devlin in the rearview mirror. "You're not what you seem, Mr. Devlin," he said.

"I don't strike you as someone who would order pizza?"

"Not at Burger King."

Devlin looked at Jimmy, smiling at his insight. "Pull forward," he said.

The limo pulled up to the window, and the girl handed Jimmy a bag and then thrust a pizza box in front of his face. He took it and handed it back to Devlin.

"Light snack," commented Jimmy.

"There's a rule I've learned to follow," Devlin said. "Don't let anyone know too much. But you're right, I'm not what I seem. I'm a secret government agent."

That certainly shut Jimmy up for a moment. Finally he found some words. "Get outta here!" he said. "Stop pulling my leg!"

"I do tend to jest, don't I?" said Devlin with a smile.

His cheeseburger finished, Jimmy started up the limo and began to pull it out of the parking lot.

In the back, Devlin opened the pizza box and took out a metallic envelope. Jimmy sneaked a glance into the rearview mirror.

"Stop!" shouted Devlin.

Jimmy whipped his eyes back to the windshield, just in time to notice a skateboarder rolling by in front of the car. He hit the brakes, and the limo screeched to a stop.

"Sorry, dude," Jimmy said under his breath to the skateboarder.

In the instant they were stopped, though, something else was going on. Unnoticed by Jimmy, another skater passed behind the limo, deftly sticking a small package to the bumper.

As the limo accelerated into the street, the skateboarder behind the car kicked up his board, slapped a different package onto it, and shoved it into the street. The skateboard began rolling along after the limo.

Devlin looked through the rear window and saw the skateboarder standing there without his board. "They know," he said urgently. "Get us out of here."

"What?" said Jimmy.

"Punch it!"

Jimmy checked his side mirrors and, just for a flashing instant, thought he saw a skateboard following them. He hit the accelerator.

Jimmy threaded in and out of traffic, and the skateboard followed, streaking under cars, nearly crushed by tires, but continuing like a shark after its prey.

A car just ahead suddenly changed lanes, forcing Jimmy to swerve out of the way. There was nothing to do but make a sharp left turn.

Uh-oh: dead end.

The skateboard made the turn right behind the trapped limo and began closing in. "Out!" cried Devlin. "Run!" He threw his door open a second before Jimmy jumped.

The skateboard rolled under the limo and exploded in a ball of fire. Limousine shrapnel filled the air.

Jimmy dove behind some stacks of cardboard boxes, and Devlin jumped behind some barrels. A sharp, sudden blow hit them a second later.

When the reverberations had stopped, Jimmy stood up shakily. "What was that? Mr. Devlin?"

Devlin stood up behind the car. "Good thing I ducked," he said. He smiled, and then collapsed back behind the car. Jimmy ran to him and found Devlin still clutching the metallic envelope. When he turned his head, Jimmy saw that there was a very nasty cut on his temple.

"Got an aspirin on you?" Devlin asked in a woozy voice.

"Stay down. You'll be okay," Jimmy told him. He pulled out his cell phone and began dialing 911.

"No police," Devlin protested. "Don't...trust anybody."

"Do you know who did this?" Jimmy asked him. The 911 operator answered. "I need an ambulance right now," he said into the phone.

Devlin was trying to say something. "Walter...Strider..." he mumbled.

"Walter Strider?" asked Jimmy, bending down to hear better. "He's the one?"

"*Walter* Strider—"

"A man is badly hurt," Jimmy said to the operator. "His name—"

Devlin held out his wallet, open to his identification. He pressed the corner of the wallet, and, weirdly, the identification began to morph before Jimmy's eyes. The clothes in the photo turned to tweed, and the address transformed itself to 543 Steward Avenue, Canton, Ohio.

"His name is...Brad Dillford," said Jimmy into the phone, his eyes popping as the new name appeared. "Get here fast."

At the hospital, Jimmy could only watch help-lessly as the semiconscious Clark was put onto a gurney and hustled toward an operating room.

"Wah-ter..." he mumbled to Jimmy.

"I will find Walter Strider. I promise," Jimmy told him.

"Please go to the waiting room!" a nurse snapped at him.

The gurney was pushed through the operating room doors. Jimmy waited a moment, watching it disappear, and then walked back down the long corridor.

In the waiting room, Jimmy sat holding Devlin's personal effects—there was a watch, and a St. Christopher medal engraved with the words TRUST NOBODY. And there was the metallic envelope.

He turned the envelope in his hands, fascin-ated. He held it up to the light, shook it, and then, unable to resist, pried open one of the seals. He changed his mind. Then he turned the envelope and pried open the other seal.

Pfoooom! The envelope went up in smoke. The woman sitting next to him gave him an odd look.

Just then a nurse walked by. "There's no smoking in here," she scolded.

"I was nervous." he said. "How is he?"

"It's touch and go. He'll be in here for a while. You might want to bring him some familiar items, anything to make him feel more comfortable when he regains consciousness."

"I'll try," said Jimmy.

"Oh, he had this clutched in his hand. I don't know if it means anything." The nurse handed him a square of paper. Jimmy unfolded it and found himself gazing at the sketch Devlin had made in the car. It appeared to be a long-legged insect.

7

That night, in a basement forensics lab not far away, four people were walking quickly down a corridor. They were Chalmers, who was a former field agent turned administrator; his two operatives, Randall, and Joel; and Steena, who looked striking, as usual, in a severe suit.

"It's a shame Devlin couldn't fit us into his busy schedule," Chalmers was grousing.

"I left messages," Randall told him.

"Why?" said Chalmers. "He doesn't pick them up."

"He probably took off for Barbados," said Joel.

Chalmers did not look amused. "As long as he didn't go black tie," he said.

"He saves that for special occasions," said Steena.

They were in the autopsy room now. A corpse lying on a steel table was wheeled out by a young forensic analyst named Gabe.

On the table lay the man who had been plastic-bagged at the bottling plant.

"Mr. Chalmers," Gabe greeted them.

"All right, fine," said Chalmers impatiently. "What do you know?"

"In simplest terms," Gabe explained, "Wallace drowned. In his bathtub."

Chalmers noticed that there was another forensic analyst moving about in the background, cleaning some beakers. It was someone he didn't know.

"A contusion here," Gabe continued, pointing to Wallace's head, "suggests that he hit his head and fell unconscious—"

Joel shook his head disbelievingly. "The man infiltrated a Serbian death squad and never got a scratch. He goes down in his bathtub?"

"Life stinks," said Chalmers. "Cover the poor bastard up." He turned to go.

"He didn't drown, sir," a woman's voice cut in. It was the other forensic analyst. Despite her serious glasses and buttoned-up appearance, she was better looking than most forensic analysts Chalmers knew. "He was murdered. Does that make life stink a little less?"

Chalmers turned. "And you would be?"

"That's Del Blaine, sir," said Gabe before she could speak again. "We're having a filter installed between her brain and mouth next week."

Chalmers ignored him. "You don't think he drowned," he said to Del.

Gabe looked at her, willing her to keep quiet.

Del ignored him, too. "Well, sir," she explained, "there was water in his lungs, but the pulmonary vein was filled with collapsed platelets, indicative of dehydration. He died of thirst."

"*Thirst?*" Chalmers echoed.

"And it wasn't city tap water," Del went on. "The mineral profile fit a high-end bottled water, but what was really weird was it contained a strain of bacteria that I so far haven't been able to culture. Anyway, I didn't mean to interrupt." She went back to washing beakers.

"You seem to know a lot about water," Chalmers said as he approached Del. "I have a special situation in the field that could use your talents," he said to her. "Interested?"

Del thought about it for about zero seconds. "When do I start?" she said.

"Ever heard of Clark Devlin?" Chalmers asked her.

"Rumors and innuendo," she replied.

"And so much more," added Steena, her voice loaded with meaning.

"Save it for the locker room, Steena," said Chalmers. He turned to Del. "Meet me upstairs in an hour," he said.

Chalmers turned and headed down the corridor, followed by Steena, Randall and Joel.

Gabe looked at Del. "One thing about you, Blaine, you don't let anyone get in the way of your ambition," he said sourly.

"I didn't sign up with the CSA to wash beakers and go home smelling of formaldehyde. What kind of life is that?"

"Mine?" Gabe reminded her. "I don't think we'll be having dinner tonight."

"Why? Do you not feel well?" asked Del.

"You eviscerated me in front of my boss!" Gabe said.

She was unruffled. "You're a great guy, Gabe, but you rushed the autopsy," she said.

"Chalmers didn't even say good-bye to me," Gabe said miserably.

"Your ego can't be that fragile."

"I'm glad you're taking that field job. People will shoot at you."

"Well, let's hope they're all as incompetent as you, sweetie."

Their dinner date was definitely off.

8

That night, all the lights were on in Clark Devlin's bedroom. Jimmy was gathering up some belongings to take to his boss in the hospital.

Opening a drawer, he spotted an address book. He took it out and turned to "S."

"Schiffer, Schwarzkopf, Sondheim, Spring-steen, Steinbrenner, Stephanopoulos, Sting..." he muttered to himself, running his finger down the names. "No Strider."

He closed the book, tossed it into a valise, and went to the closet. He was wearing Devlin's St. Christopher medal and watch.

Inside the closet, he opened a drawer and pulled out a pair of pajamas. He took a robe from a hanger. Then something seemed to beckon him, to pull at his attention. It was the tuxedo.

Hanging in its glass case, it almost seemed to be glowing. Jimmy moved toward it, all alone with it now. He reached for the door and as he did, the face of the watch lit up with the same ethereal glow. As if guided by some force, Jimmy's hand moved to the watch and pressed a button. Nothing. He pressed another button. Nothing. He pressed two buttons simultaneously. The glass doors rose like a curtain. There was the tuxedo, naked. Jimmy reached out and carefully touched the lapel.

"Wow," Jimmy whispered, awestruck.

In less than a minute, Jimmy was wearing the tux. He admired himself in a mirror. "It fits!" he exclaimed, pleasantly surprised. He looked cool, except for the bow tie, which hung in a lank knot. Jimmy never could tie a tie.

He shot his cuffs, which made him notice the watch. On the face were two tiny words. He squinted to see them:

OFF.

ON.

Carefully, he pressed a button on the watch. The ON button blinked. He pressed the other button.

Shoom! The tux immediately straightened up, as if a rod had just been shoved up Jimmy's spine. The lines of the suit were perfect now, the creases razor sharp.

If Jimmy had thought he looked cool before, now he looked awesome. His posture was perfect. He was even taller.

Without any orders from Jimmy, his hands flew to the bow tie and whipped it into a perfect knot in two seconds flat. His hands had never moved so fast. What was going on?

He lifted the coat to have a look at the lining, and found that it was made of a fabric with a geometric pattern. He looked closer, and then closer still.

The lining was a complex circuit board.

The label on the inside pocket confirmed his wildest imaginings: TACTICAL UNIFORM EXPERIMENT, IT SAID. CSA REQ. NO. 187-007-2583, PROPERTY OF U.S. GOV'T.

He examined the label on the other side. FORTY-TWO LONG, it said.

Buttoning the jacket, he now noticed that the watch face was glowing, displaying a rapidly scrolling list of undecipherable data. He pushed a button and a new list began scrolling down the screen. This one he could read. "Chess," he read. "Chromatograph...DNA Fingerprinting..."

He scrolled to KUNG FU, feeling that at that moment he'd rather know how to defend himself than how to tap dance. He was ready, but nothing happened.

Ah, there was a sub-menu. He scrolled down through the words: ATTACK...DEFEND...DEMO.

"Demo. Okay. Show me," he said aloud. He hit the EXECUTE button, noticing just a second too late that on the watch face, DEMO was highlighted, but on the line below it, it said LITION.

DEMOLITION.

"Uh-oh," said Jimmy.

His head snapped back from the sudden acceleration as he bounded across the room, rising into the air to flying-kick the flat-screen TV.

He whirled and sidestepped toward the glass collection, struggling to physically control the tuxedo, but there was no fighting it. With slashing hands, he turned the a whole collection of crystal to glistening rubble. He crushed a collection of Fabergé eggs. He flung CDs like ninja throwing stars. He punched holes in a priceless Winslow Homer painting.

Ricocheting off a wall, he grabbed a chair and flipped it over his head and through a window. Then he did handsprings across the room to the bed and demolished it with ease.

"Oops...Sorry...pardon me...excuse me..." he gibbered as he was flung around the room by the tuxedo. "I'll fix that...my bad...I'll replace those."

Frantically, he tried to remove the jacket as he bounced around. He managed to pull his right arm free and used it to grab hold of his left arm to stop it from smashing the stereo equipment. His arms struggled mightily against each other.

He propelled himself to a door, opened it, and slammed it onto his left arm, leaning against the door to keep the arm immobilized. But the arm smashed through the door and grabbed him by the throat.

Jimmy flailed against his own attacking arm. Frenzied, he pressed the buttons on the watch, trying to press STOP. But what he hit instead was the button that said SPIDER.

Suddenly, he let go of himself and started reeling backward, into a wall and then up it. He was scuttling upward like a three-legged tarantula, his unsleeved arm useless in the situation. Finally he stuck his arm into the other sleeve, and crawled up the wall and across the ceiling.

Over the intercom came the butler's voice. "Mr. Devlin? Is everything all right?"

"Oh, hello! It's Jimmy," said Jimmy in a manically cheerful voice. "He asked me to ask you if tomorrow you could spend a few minutes straightening up his room. It got messy somehow."

"As soon as he is awake," said the butler.

"Maybe after he leaves. Thanks."

What now? A cell phone was ringing. For a moment, Jimmy couldn't figure out the source, but he quickly he realized that it was coming from the tuxedo. He took both hands off the ceiling to feel his pockets, and plummeted downward, flipping backward once and hitting the floor flat. A tiny cell phone bounced out of his pocket and skittered across the floor, still ringing.

Painfully, he reached out and picked up the phone, not sure whether to answer. But what was one more risk, after he'd taken so many? What the heck. He pushed TALK.

"...Hello?" he said tentatively.

"Are we on?" It was a woman's voice.

"Are we on what?" said Jimmy.

"I think I must have the wrong number." It was a young woman's voice.

"You are calling Clark Devlin," Jimmy said.

In the CSA office, Del had a folder open in front of her. "Why are you using that ridiculous accent?" she asked.

Jimmy was taken aback. "This is how I talk."

"Fine. You're the senior officer, Mr. Devlin. I'll play it however you want."

Jimmy's face lit with understanding. "I'm Clark Devlin?" he said.

"If we can please get down to business, sir,

Diedrich Banning is holding a meeting of international CEOs aboard his boat. Chalmers wants surveillance."

Jimmy thought fast. "And what about Walter Strider?"

"Who is he?" asked the woman.

"I don't know." replied Jimmy.

"Okay...more time wasted. Now, we'll meet tonight, eight o'clock at Pier Seventeen at the base of the silo," Del continued, reading with distaste from the file,

"Eight o'clock," Jimmy confirmed.

"Very funny. And listen, Mr. Devlin, as you know, this is my first time in the field. I don't expect to be coddled but, well, I'm sure you can remember your first assignment."

"Yes. I know just how you feel," said Jimmy truthfully.

"See you later." She clicked off.

9

That night Jimmy took the sports car. He nervously checked his watch for the umpteenth time. Three minutes after eight.

As the car approached the silo, Jimmy looked through the windshield. There, illuminated in the headlights, was Del Blaine. He checked himself over; everything was zipped and buttoned.

"Hello. Clark Devlin," he said, practicing. "Good evening. They call me Clark Devlin..."

She was coming toward the car. He got out.

Del stopped, watching him coming toward her. Backlit by the headlights, he formed an impressive silhouette.

She talked fast, already totally amped. "We've got five minutes to get into position. 1 secured the rooftop, the equipment's good to go, and 1 have to say it's a great honor to be working with the legendary—"

Now she saw his face in the light.

"Clark Devlin?" She stared at him, confused, and then caught herself. "I'm Del Blaine."

"Have we met before?" Jimmy asked her.

"No."

"Good," he said, relieved. "Okay, Delblaine. Let's do what we came here to do."

"I'll follow you," she said.

"Ladies first."

She hesitantly walked toward the silo stairs. He followed, relieved that she appeared to have bought his act.

"A couple details changed from what was in the file." When he looked perplexed, she said, "You read it, right?"

"Files are crap," said Jimmy gruffly, covering. "Give me the short version."

"Diedrich Banning's holding a meeting with nine international water company CEOs," she said, leading as they climbed the stairs to the top. "We've been tracking him for six years. A couple weeks ago the agent heading the operation was found, his internal organs shriveled, his eyeballs deflated—"

"Was he sick?" said Jimmy, clueless.

"Dead. So now you're the man."

Jimmy nodded, quite troubled at this news.

"Anyway," she concluded, "Chalmers wants to know what's going down at this meeting."

Del snapped open an attaché case. Inside were binoculars, headphones, and a listening receiver. She handed Jimmy the case. "Here you go," she said.

Jimmy looked at the case, turned it in his hand, opened it, and looked at all the stuff inside. Then he turned it and opened the other side. Inside was a sniper rifle, disassembled.

"Klineholtz silenced bolt-action 9-mm, titanium folding stock with 20x infrared sniper scope and counterweighted micro-rifled barrel," she informed him.

"My favorite gun," said Jimmy. "But I don't kill people anymore."

She took a small transmitter projectile from a box. "You're not killing anyone. You're planting a bug. It was all in that crap file."

Jimmy picked up the pieces as if he was staring at a jigsaw puzzle. She watched him.

"Go look through your binoculars," Jimmy told her.

As Del moved to the edge of the silo, Jimmy pressed the button on his watch, scrolling the index to ASSEMBLE WEAPON.

Up the tuxedo sleeve, fine probes touched the skin of his forearm, sending impulses traveling down his nerve pathways. His hands plucked up parts, and twisted, snapped, and screwed them together. It was incredible. Jimmy was amazed by his own dexterity and speed.

"They're arriving," Del said.

She looked back to see him holding the completed rifle. He casually blew a speck of dust from the scope. "Let's rock and roll," he said.

He joined her at the edge of the silo.

"Aim for the briefcase," she said.

Jimmy gave her an I-know-what-I'm-doing look and raised the rifle. Unfortunately, it trembled noticeably.

"What's the matter?" she said.

"Too much wind. Turn around and bend over," he instructed.

She started to follow his command, but then stopped and turned back to face him. "Time out," she said. "Let me be really clear about this. I may be the rookie and you're the veteran pro, but I'm not impressed by power under any circumstances."

"Me either," said Jimmy innocently.

"Steena told me all about how you operate."

"Who?" said Jimmy.

Del was scandalized. "*Ah!* You don't even remember her name."

"It was a long time ago."

"Last *month*?"

"Oh! Steena! She's the one who pays me."

Now Del was truly disgusted. "Let's just keep this professional."

"I am. I need a tripod."

She finally got the reason for his bizarre request. "*Oh!* A tripod. Sure," she said, turning and hunkering down. "Like this?"

He rested the barrel on her shoulder and looked into the scope. He could see the deck of Banning's boat, and Banning's guards ushering the water company executives aboard.

Jimmy, of course, was not used to holding a high-powered rifle, and he could not keep the crosshairs from jumping all over the place. He looked away from the scope to the watch, madly pressing buttons in an effort to find some tuxedo action that would help. "Aiming, shooting, trigger, come on," he whispered at it.

"What're you doing?" said Del, still bending over. "Hurry up!"

"I'm the commander. I do it my way!" Jimmy looked into the scope again, holding his breath. The rifle trembled as his finger twitched on the trigger.

He fired.

The silenced muzzle flashed. It had not been loud, but Del flinched.

A guard who was hanging around near the ship's railing was struck in the temple. Jimmy recognized him as one of the skateboarders from the other night. The guard fell into the water, unnoticed by the others.

Del looked through the binoculars. She gasped, but then remembered she was the junior agent and regained her cool. "You kind of missed," she said.

"You flinched," said Jimmy.

"Of course I flinched. A gun went off in my ear!"

"Not professional," said Jimmy, shaking his head.

"Sorry. I guess I missed tripod class back at the academy."

"Let's go," Jimmy said. He'd had enough of this secret agent business.

"We have to plant the bug!" insisted Del. She took out another projectile transmitter.

He snatched it from her and she clamped a pair of headphones on her ears. "Turn around," he said.

"What?"

"Turn around!" He was shouting now.

"Better luck this time, *commander*," she said sarcastically under her breath.

"I can hear you!" he said.

She turned and trained her binoculars on the executives on the boat. Meanwhile, Jimmy scrolled the watch until he found a line that said SNIPER MODE. He pressed the button. The tuxedo instantly dropped him into a kneeling position, as rigid as steel. He swung the rifle barrel down, swiftly and surely.

Like a seasoned pro, he looked through the scope as the crosshairs swung the across the line of executives and stopped dead on a briefcase.

Del glanced at Jimmy, impressed by his sudden rock-solid calm.

His finger squeezed the trigger and the rifle silently recoiled. The bullet left the muzzle, rocketing toward the briefcase. The projectile transmitter hit the briefcase this time, but then ricocheted off a gold latch, and buried itself in the bun worn in the hair of an executive. She started down the stairs into the hold with the group, completely unaware of what had landed in her hair. Jimmy lowered the rifle, a proud smile on his face. "He shoots, he scores!" he whooped.

"*Shush!*" said Del.

Jimmy thought the job was over, but Del knew better. She was listening intently on the headphones.

—◼—

Down in the boat's hold, nine executives, all owners of international water companies, were gathered. The lights dimmed.

Large video screens rose, immediately filled with magnificent, swirling video images of Niagara

Falls, rushing streams, gushing geysers, and azure lakes. Banning gazed at it all lovingly.

"Aqua," he said, "*agua, miza, eau, Wasser...* water." On the screen, the images shifted. Now there were shots of bottled water factories, delivery trucks, children, housewives, doctors, and athletes—all drinking bottled water.

"In the year 2001," Banning said to the group, "thirty-five billion dollars' worth of bottled water was consumed worldwide. Today, bottled water costs more per gallon than gasoline. We, my friends, are the new oil barons."

The executives applauded.

Now the bottled water on the screen clouded up and turned a foul, mottled ochre. "But very soon," Banning went on, "a combination of global warming, toxic waste, and overpopulation will affect even your sources."

The executives looked shocked and angry.

"And that is why I have brought you here," he continued. "To save you."

◼

Up on the deck, Kells and another thug named Rogers were standing guard. Kells glanced up to the top of the silo, and the other man followed his eyes.

"Pigeons," said Rogers quietly.

Kells nodded.

✖

Downstairs, Banning was ramming his message home. "I've invested millions to perfect a filtration process that extracts pure fresh water from the toxic filth which will pour forth from your sources," he told the group. "I want to share my brainchild with you."

Kells materialized beside Banning and motioned to interrupt him. Banning was really rolling now and didn't want to break his flow, so he tried to ignore the interruption. But Kells was insistent. Finally Banning broke off. "Digest this information a moment," he told his audience. Then he turned to Kells. "What?" he hissed.

Kells bent down and spoke softly to Banning.

✖

On top of the silo, Del pressed the headphones to her ears.

"What are they saying?" Jimmy wanted to know.

Del turned up the volume on her receiver and pressed the headphones harder. "He was talking about his filtration process," she said. "But now I can barely make it out...someone's saying, 'There are two of them. We're taking care of it now.' What do you think that means?"

They did not have to puzzle over it for long, because at that instant a climbing rope was thrown over Jimmy's head from behind. He was knocked off his feet and set upon by two of Banning's men.

Desperately, he tried to voice-activate the tuxedo. "Fight! Attack! Kung fu!" he yelled.

But when he glanced at the watch, the message on the face read, VOICE UNKNOWN.

"It's me!" Jimmy yelled at it. He tried to activate the tuxedo manually, but his hand was inexplicably pulled away every time his finger came close to the watch's buttons. Meanwhile, he was definitely getting beaten up.

"I think we should go," he said to Del.

But Del was busy looking at the boat. She shook her head, half in negation and half in terror.

"No?" said Jimmy. Then he turned and saw what she saw.

Six very large and very bad guys were headed toward them.

With a mighty effort, Jimmy broke free of his two assailants. He lunged for the first bad guy in this new group and knocked him backward past Del, who grabbed the rifle and swung it at him. But he was quick and strong. He caught the rifle easily with one hand and hurled it off the silo, spinning Del halfway around.

Del squared off in front of the man, boxing

style. "Training manual Chapter Six, unarmed assailant, frontal attack—" she recited to herself.

She thrust the heel of her hand against his chin. He smiled and grabbed her by the hair, putting her in a headlock. So much for Chapter Six.

"Choke hold defense..." Del grunted, trying to remember what to do in the present situation. Finally she had it. "Oh, yeah!" she said, proceeding to stomp on his foot. Nothing. She did it again. Nothing.

"Okay, let's try Chapter Seven," she said.

Meanwhile, Jimmy was throwing punches at the next two bad guys in the pack, who had ducked around some pipes to come at him.

Del elbowed her bad guy in the stomach and then in the groin. He merely tightened his hold.

"According to the manual," Del choked, "you are now unconscious."

He just tossed her around a little harder. She tried backhanding him in the face. No effect.

"What manual did you read?" she panted.

Elsewhere on the roof, Jimmy had made some headway with his bad guys. He was tying up two of them with the rope.

Del made an executive decision. "Screw the manual!" she said, and bit her bad guy on the arm. He yelped and threw her down.

Jimmy ran over to help Del and was punched back toward the pipes.

Now Del and her bad guy were down, and Jimmy and another bad guy were up. A four-person chain reaction of kicking ensued, knocking Jimmy's bad guy out and sending Jimmy hurtling toward the railing at the edge of the silo.

Rebounding off the rail, Jimmy stomped on Del's bad guy's hand. The man screamed and thrust his hand up, sending Jimmy flipping over the rail.

Just in time, Jimmy grabbed the top rail, but the man pulled Jimmy's hand off. Jimmy grabbed the middle rail with his other hand. The man kicked it off. In desperation, Jimmy grabbed the bottom rail with his free hand and punched the thug from in between the rails, knocking him off to the side.

Just as the man was getting up to attack again, Del whip-kicked him, knocking him flat. "Class dismissed!" she yelled at him.

Now she had to deal with the problem of Jimmy, who was still dangling from the railing. She grabbed his hand and tried to haul him back up, but his weight dragged her toward the rail.

"Let me go!" Jimmy said.

"And have that on my resume?" she retorted.

Just as her sleeve ripped off in Jimmy's hand,

he grabbed her other hand. She braced herself, struggling not to be pulled over.

And, as if this were not enough, the bad guys were still coming. They were heading toward Del, looking mean. Meanwhile, Jimmy was down to holding onto Del's finger.

Her ring slipped off in his hand.

Over the edge went Jimmy, while Del was sent reeling backward into the pack of onrushing thugs.

Jimmy plummeted through the air, screaming. On the silo roof, Del sprinted to a ladder and started climbing down, the goons right behind her.

"Being Clark Devlin," howled Jimmy on his way down to being flattened, "*sucks!*"

That seemed to be the magic word. As if given a command, the tuxedo whipped into action. It suctioned itself to a thick pipe and began clambering upward.

Del, climbing down the ladder as Jimmy climbed up the pipe, passed him in the dark. They didn't see each other.

When Jimmy reached the top, he looked for Del. All he saw were a few scattered bodies of knocked-out bad guys. He headed for the ladder, but more of the hoods were now coming across a catwalk toward him. There was no way he would get to the ladder before they reached him. He looked for an escape. *Ah-ha*. He had it.

As the men ran across the catwalk, they suddenly found that they had lost sight of Jimmy. This was because he was hanging underneath, moving hand-over-hand across it, like a kid on monkey bars. On the far side, he spotted a pipe and slid down it, only to land in an open cement truck.

◄►

Meanwhile, in the hold of Banning's boat, the meeting was still going on. Banning stood in front of the screens, which now showed images of scientists and intricate machinery. "You have heard all I have to say," he said to the CEOs. "Now I would like to hear from you."

A hand was raised in the back.

"Yes?" said Banning.

Simms rose to his feet at the back of the group. Banning, seeing him, looked annoyed.

"You said your filtration process 'extracts' pure water," said Simms, "but I believe you meant to say that toxic elements in solution are converted to negative ions which are electromagnetically attracted to an anode grid, leaving H_2O molecules in an unsaturated state."

"I stand corrected," said Banning.

Simms sat back down, sulking that he hadn't been introduced.

"Any other questions?" Banning asked the group.

Simms's hand went up again.

Banning was really irritated now. "Yes!" he snapped.

Simms stood once more. "I'm proud to have played a small, unacknowledged role in the development of this revolutionary process," he announced. "I would be happy to answer any technical questions that might arise."

"Thank you...Dr. Simms," said Banning through gritted teeth.

"You are welcome," said Simms. Somewhat satisfied, he sat down.

"If there are no more questions—" said Banning.

An executive named Rollins spoke up. "How much will your scheme cost us?" he asked.

"You always go straight to the heart of the matter, Frank," said Banning. There was laughter from the others. "Not a dime out of pocket," he told them. "All I ask is to become your slightly more-than-equal partner."

Rollins immediately stood up and headed for the exit. "My family's been in business seventy years," he said over his shoulder. "You're going to tell my dad and me how to make water? Dream on, Banning."

"Call my office if you reconsider," Banning called after him.

Outside, Rollins strode angrily toward the line of limos. "Get my car," he said to Rogers, who was waiting near the exit.

"Your driver said he'd be back after the meeting," Rogers told him. "Don't worry, I'll get you a ride, Mr. Rollins."

Rogers motioned for a limo, and Rollins got into the backseat.

"Have a nice trip," Rogers muttered as the limo pulled away.

❧

Now perched on the edge of the cement truck, Jimmy was using a security light to try to signal Del, who was climbing down the ladder. But before he could make contact, a chunk of debris from the fight on the roof fell down and beaned him, knocking him off his perch and sending him falling back into the cement truck.

Del reached the bottom of the ladder, ran to Jimmy's car, jumped in, and peeled away.

Jimmy climbed out of the truck, covered in gray dust. The tuxedo shook itself clean like a wet dog.

A minute later, Del pulled up in his car, leaned over, and opened the passenger door without a word. Jimmy got in. As she accelerated away, clouds of dust blew from his face and hair.

They reached the parking lot, and she pulled

up next to her own car. She got out and slammed the door.

"Are you upset?" Jimmy asked her.

"Why would I be upset? I've always wanted to begin and end my career with a big, fat failure. Thank you very much, Mr. Devlin."

Jimmy followed her toward her car. "But I saved your life," he protested.

"In what parallel universe?" she shot back.

"A lot of guys were trying to kill us...or am I wrong about that, too?"

"Forgive me if I seem hypercritical," Del said. "I realize you've got this rogue-agent reputation to uphold but we might have succeeded in the mission if you'd gone a little more by the book. I take that back—if you had *read* the book."

"It's my first time," Jimmy said, then he caught himself. "I mean, every mission is like the first time."

She was softening a little bit, he could see it.

"It's not so easy being Clark Devlin," he said, meaning it. He turned to go to his car.

Del felt bad. She moved after him and reached out to touch his shoulder. But the tuxedo's automatic defense mode kicked in, causing Jimmy to whirl and execute a perfect judo throw. Del landed at his feet.

"I didn't do that!" he yelped.

"What's the matter with you?" she yelped back.

"I'm not who you think I am," Jimmy said helplessly.

He tried to help her up, but she sprang to her feet, on guard. "I'm a little overamped right now myself," she said, "so let's call it a day." She turned to leave. "Get some rest...and medication," she added under her breath.

"Say what?"

"We'll be in communication," she said, covering herself.

Jimmy watched Del get into her car. "I don't have your phone number," he said.

Without another word, she drove away.

◆

In the backseat of the limo Roberts had called for him, bottled-water owner Rollins took out his cell phone to make a call. The screen read No Service.

He opened a side cabinet, took out a whiskey decanter and glass, and poured himself a stiff drink.

He moved his feet, puzzled by an odd sort of squishy sound from below. Had he spilled the whiskey? He turned on a reading light.

"Hey, your refrigerator's leaking," Rollins called up front to the driver.

The driver was Kells.

Kells raised the privacy glass and flipped a switch under the dash, whereupon water began gushing out of the air-conditioning vents in the back. Rollins watched in horror as it flooded into the watertight passenger compartment. He tried to open the door; he tried to lower the window; he kicked at the privacy glass. Nothing worked. The water rose and rose.

❧

On the ship, Banning bade good-bye to the executives. "Call me with any questions...Thank you for your trust," he was saying amiably. "I look forward to a profitable partnership. Hey, you like James Brown? I'm going to see him Friday and I'd love you to join me," he said to one of them.

As they were leaving, he saw Rogers approaching with some of his thugs, who were all looking rather beaten up.

"Excuse me," Banning said to the last guests. He went to Rogers, who was carrying Del's and Jimmy's rifle case and listening equipment.

Banning looked at the equipment. "You don't pick this up at the surplus store," he mused.

"Kells can track them," Rogers said. "They'll be dead by dinnertime."

"Not until we know what they know," Banning said grimly.

10

At the CSA shooting range, someone was aiming the blue steel barrel of a nine-millimeter Beretta at a man-shaped target. It was Steena. She wore shooting glasses and ear protectors. Her hair, which was usually arranged into a tight bun, fell loosely over her shoulders.

She racked the slide, chambering a cartridge. Then she raised the gun to firing position and squeezed the trigger.

The muzzle flashed with the repeated explosions: *Bam bam bam bam! Bam bam bam bam!*

Steena lowered the gun. She and Del were the only ones out on the shooting range. Two guys in CSA windbreakers watched them from inside on monitors, considering whether to go out and flirt with them.

"Who am I kidding?" Del was saying to Steena. "I have no idea what I'm doing or why I'm doing it."

"I felt exactly the same way when I took my first field assignment," Steena said. "And then I met Clark Devlin." She slapped a fresh magazine into the gun and handed it to Del. "He made the lights go on," she added.

Del took a shooting stance and fired off a few shots, flinching with each blast. "Everybody warned me he was unorthodox," she said when she was done, "but he's very irrational, bordering on nuts."

Steena now had a MAC 10 .45-caliber full auto. She blazed away at another target, blowing big holes in the head and chest.

The two guys watching on monitors shrank away a little.

"He's getting under your skin, isn't he?" Steena said to Del. "He got under my skin once. I still have the scars."

"Yeah, I know, you told me. It's not as interesting the fourth time. Get over it."

"No, you're right," Steena agreed.

Steena blew away the target's groin. That is when the two guys decided to go get a beer and watch football.

"And what about his English?" Del said.

"I know. I never could understand half of what he said. Don't you love his accent?"

"I got used to it," said Del.

Steena checked to make sure they were alone, and then handed Del a metallic envelope.

"Another assignment with him?" said Del.

"Devlin may not be your type," Steena said to her, "but he can teach you a lot, if you're open to learning."

"He almost got us *killed*."

Steena shrugged. "What's better than escaping death?"

Del smiled a little. "I have to say, we kicked some serious butt. I mean, what a rush!"

Now Steena pulled out an even bigger gun, a full-auto AK-47.

"God, I wish I were back in the field," said Steena. She fired off the big gun, ripping the target to confetti.

The sports car was parked outside a low-rent apartment building. Kids clustered around it, peeking in through its windows.

Inside, Jimmy was at Mitch's apartment, which they had formerly shared. It was basically one large room and it was a total mess.

"While you are off living like a prince," Mitch was saying, "I am driving eighteen hours a day to pay rent."

"So get another roommate," Jimmy said.

"Who would want to live in this pigsty?" said Mitch.

"Clean it up."

"For three weeks it has been your turn to clean, not mine," Mitch complained.

"Mitch, just tell me, did your cousin find out anything about Walter Strider?"

"Yes, yes. I wrote it down. Where did I put it?"

Mitch went and searched through a small desk in the hall. Jimmy moved toward the kitchen area.

"Charmain searched the DMV computers for the Northeast, the Southwest, the Northwest, the Southeast, and Hawaii," Mitch continued. "She said 'Mitch, there are privacy laws.' I said, 'This is for my friend Jimmy, break the damn laws, woman.' *Ah!* Here it is." Mitch unfolded a computer printout and walked back into the room, not noticing that it was now neat as a robin's egg. "It seems that your Walter Strider—"

Mitch looked up to see the perfectly clean room. Jimmy casually wiped a glass and put it in the cupboard.

"You are very fast," Mitch observed.

"I know. Now what about Strider?" asked Jimmy impatiently.

"It seems he does not exist. No car, no credit cards, no phone."

"I have to find him," said Jimmy. "I promised Mr. Devlin."

Just then, Jimmy's cell phone rang, and Jimmy and Mitch jumped. Jimmy pulled out his cell phone and walked to one side of the room for some privacy. "Hello?" he said to the cell phone.

"Guess who's dead?" said Del's voice.

"Walter Strider?" guessed Jimmy.

Del was calling from the CSA. Gabe was

hanging around her desk, but she didn't want to talk to him.

"I don't know who that is," Del said to Jimmy, "but no, Frank Rollins, he was at Banning's meeting. What's your take on it?"

"Who's the student and who's the teacher here? You tell me," said Jimmy, vamping for all he was worth.

"Rollins didn't go for Banning's takeover scheme," Del said, "so he eliminated him. He's reaching critical mass."

Del was all business. She studiously avoided Gabe, who was desperately trying to get her attention. He held up a piece of paper, on which he'd drawn a cute smiley face.

"Not bad. You're learning. What is the next move?"

Del pulled up her skirt. A Beretta pistol was strapped to her thigh. She began polishing it. Gabe held up another piece of paper that read, "I'm sorry."

"After the fiasco with planting the bug," Del said to Jimmy, "I'd say we have no choice but to go to level-one surveillance."

"In other words..."

"Infiltration," said Del. "Banning's going to be at the Landford Hotel tonight entertaining three of his new partners. Chalmers has arranged for us to be at the next table."

Gabe held up a final piece of paper with a sweet little heart. When Del ignored that, too, he decided to leave.

"This is a black-tie event?" asked Jimmy hopefully.

"No, but I'm sure you'll wear whatever you want. I'll meet you there at eight."

"See you," said Jimmy.

"Whatever you say, sir."

They hung up.

"Was that Walter Strider?" Mitch asked Jimmy.

"Some questions," Jimmy said darkly, "I can't answer. Understand?"

Mitch nodded.

"That was a woman I'm involved with," said Jimmy. "Can't say any more."

"Okay," said Mitch.

Jimmy couldn't stand it. "Taking her to a party. That's all I can tell you."

Mitch nodded again.

"Going to see James Brown at the Landford Hotel. Meeting her at eight."

"Fine," chuckled Mitch, "keep your secrets. But tell me this—do you have a minute to do the laundry?" He noticed the look Jimmy was giving him. "No? All right. Have fun."

12

The Landford Hotel was a posh place, all glittering lights and beautiful people—especially tonight. Cars and limos pulled up, disgorging a black-tie crowd.

Jimmy jetted to the head of the line, where eager valets descended on his car. A valet opened the door and Jimmy got out.

"Thank you," he said. "Take two spaces."

Jimmy headed for the entrance, but stopped in midstep, seeing someone. It was Del. She was radiantly beautiful, wearing a slinky blue gown. Her hair fell in soft curls.

"Delblaine," said Jimmy, knocked out.

"I know you're partial to that monkey suit of yours, so I thought I'd get gussied up," she said with a smile.

"Good job. You gussy very well," he said.

"Here's a little something for you." She took

a boutonniere from her evening bag and slid it into his lapel.

He was touched by the gesture. "Thank you," he said.

She pulled out a compact and opened it toward Jimmy, revealing not a mirror but a TV screen, on which he saw her face. "It's a camera," she explained, pointing to his boutonniere.

"Oh, good, now everybody knows," he said authoritatively. "Try to act normal, okay?"

"Sorry," said Del.

She took Jimmy's arm, and they headed toward the wide glass doors, looking just like the most beautiful of the "beautiful people." Everyone stared.

"Do you ever get bored of the whole rich-and-famous scene?" she asked him.

"All caviar tastes the same after awhile," Jimmy said.

"You don't have to humor me. I know you lead a charmed life," she said.

"I make it look easy, but sometimes, underneath the tuxedo, I feel like a fraud."

"A frog?" said Del, mystified.

"Fraud. Not real. Maybe because it all happened so fast. By accident."

"I heard you grew up in a wealthy family and

inherited a quarter billion, plus or minus," she questioned.

Jimmy's eyes darted as he tried to think of something to reply to this revelation. "Even birth is an accident," he finally said.

"Don't get all Obi Wan Kenobi on me."

"I didn't," said Jimmy.

Now they were inside the hotel, where a maitre d' with a list was waiting.

"What name are we under?" Jimmy asked Del quietly.

"I don't know. You're the commander. Didn't you talk to Chalmers?"

"Yes, I talked to him," said Jimmy, talking fast. "We talk all the time, because I'm Clark Devlin."

"And what did you talk about?" she inquired.

"It's top secret." *Whew*. Got out of that one.

He took Del's arm and strolled toward the maitre d'.

"Good evening," said the man.

Jimmy smiled and kept walking. "Good evening," he replied.

The maitre d' stopped him. "You have a reservation?" he asked.

"Of course. Mr. Lincoln. Right there?" Jimmy suavely pointed to the list with a folded five-dollar bill. The maitre d' looked at the pathetic sum of money and then at Jimmy with icy disdain.

Jimmy added a couple of one-dollar bills. "...And Miss Washington Washington," he added.

Jimmy smiled. The maitre d' did not.

◆

Two minutes later, they were out in the hotel alleyway, where a limo and equipment trucks were parked. Jimmy noticed a door that was slightly open, and hurried Del along. She was unsteady in her high heels and generally unhappy about the course of events.

"You're a billionaire and you try to grease the guy with *seven bucks*?" she complained.

"You think I got rich throwing my money away?" said Jimmy.

As they approached the door, a large security guard stepped out.

"Perfect," muttered Del.

"I'll talk to him," said Jimmy as the security guard moved toward them.

"No," said Del. "This time we do it my way. I've got a T-135 disorientation module. You just stand there."

Del bent and lifted her skirt to search for the device she intended to use on the security guard, while Jimmy shielded her from view. In this position, he noticed that she was breathtaking, if not downright stunning.

Jimmy stepped aside, giving the security guard a view that instantly stopped him in his tracks. A stupefied smile spread across his face.

"Your equipment worked," said Jimmy as Del looked up and saw the grinning guard.

"Smile and move," Jimmy suggested. He took her hand and pulled her past the besotted guard, who breathed in her perfume deeply.

Now they were inside, in a hallway. "We're still no closer to Banning," Del reminded Jimmy.

"One step at a time," he said.

An announcer's voice, amplified by loud-speakers, reverberated through the hallways back-stage. "Ladies and gentlemen, the Landford Hotel is proud to present a musical legend—"

They passed a dressing room. "James Brown!" cried Jimmy. He pulled Del into the doorway, and there was James Brown, ready to go onstage.

"I can't believe it!" Jimmy dithered. "The godfather of soul!"

"What's happening?" James Brown said easily.

"Forgive us for bothering you," Del, who was in better possession of her faculties. "We came to see your show—"

"She forgot to make reservations," said Jimmy, pointing to Del.

"I'll make sure they find you seats down front," said James Brown.

"Thank you so much, Mr. Brown," said Del.

"See, things work out," Jimmy said to her, pleased with himself.

James Brown looked Del up and down. "I know it's not 'in' to give compliments to the ladies," he told her, "but I have to say...nice rack."

"Thank you," said Jimmy idiotically.

"Enjoy the show," said James Brown as Jimmy and Del turned to leave. He gave Jimmy a parting slap on the shoulder, and instantly the tux was in full defense mode against an attack from the rear.

James Brown went down hard.

"Put your hands together one more time," the announcer's voice was booming from the loud-speakers, "for the hardest-working man in show business."

Jimmy and Del were both stunned.

"You killed James Brown!" Del yelled at Jimmy.

Jimmy dropped to his knees beside his victim. "He's fine," he said hopefully.

"He's not 'fine!'" Del yelled. "And Banning's leaving!"

"Don't panic," said Jimmy. He turned away and started scrolling the watch, looking for help.

"Are you praying?" Del asked him.

"Get the microphone," Jimmy ordered her. "Say James Brown isn't here. Tell the audience there will be another act. Go!"

She took off, and Jimmy quickly scrolled the watch to SING. He scrolled through the choices: BALLAD...BLUES...OPERA...RAP...ROCK...SOUL.

On stage, the lights dimmed. "Ladies and gentlemen," said Del's voice through the microphone, "James Brown..."

The applause started before she could finish. "...will not appear tonight due to unforeseen circumstances," she went on.

An unhappy murmur rippled through the audience, and Banning started to leave.

"Stay right where you are!" said Del, thinking fast, "because the Landford Hotel is proud to present the Last Emperor of Soul."

Jimmy ran onto the stage. "Hey, how are you tonight?" he greeted the crowd.

There was stony silence.

"Who wants to get funky?" he tried.

Someone in the back of the room hooted.

"All right!" said Jimmy.

Del stood to one side, looking as if she was going to be sick.

Down in the audience, Banning was looking

very unhappy. Del could see him wondering aloud to his companions, "who was this jerk."

Jimmy turned to the musicians. They were cool. As musicians, they were used to surprises. "I know I'm not James Brown," Jimmy told them, "but follow me."

Jimmy ran his hands through his hair and turned back to the audience. His hair was now in a pompadour.

Jimmy started singing one of James Brown's signature songs. "Do it with me now! Come on! Come on! Heyyy!" he yelled, gyrating madly as the musicians started playing. "Get up, get on up. Get up, get on up. Stay on the scene."

Del, watching from the wings, was open-mouthed in astonishment. She looked into the audience at Banning's table. Banning's guests, including his fiancee, a woman named Cheryl, were starting to rock out. Banning and Rogers remained somber, but at least they were not going anywhere.

"Wait a minute!" Jimmy sang. "Shake your arm, then use your form. Stay on the scene." Over his Adam's apple, the tuxedo's bow tie vibrated, sending signals into Jimmy's larynx.

Cheryl stood up and started shimmying, which annoyed Banning.

"Get up, get on up. Get up, get on up." Jimmy whooped, strutting around the stage. Half the audience was now standing up and shaking their booties.

From back in the wings, Del kept an eye on the Banning table. Jimmy looked over at her and winked. She gave him a cool nod in return.

Back in his dressing room, James Brown struggled back to consciousness. Hearing his music, he shook his head and jumped to his feet."Good Gawd!" he squawked.

He hurried down the hallway toward the stage, passing Del, who was unable stop him. Barreling onto the stage, he slid up to Jimmy. The band faltered, not quite knowing what they were supposed to do. Jimmy lowered the microphone. There was a long, loaded moment of silence between them.

Then James Brown spoke. "I hit on your girl," he said. "I deserved what I got."

Jimmy sighed with relief. "She's not my girl," he said. "It's okay."

James Brown turned to the band. "Fellas," he said, "I'm ready to get up and do my thing."

The band started up playing again.

"Stay on the scene," James Brown said to Jimmy.

Now he started singing in the way that only James Brown could sing. "Do it with me now! Come on!" he hollered. The audience went wild.

Jimmy joined in on the chorus. "Get up, get on up. Get up, get on up. Stay on the scene!" they sang together.

"You got to have the feeling sure as you're born, get it together, right on, right on." James Brown sang.

"Get up, get on up," the two of them sang. "I said the feeling you got to get. Give me the fever in a cold sweat."

James Brown did a slippery dance step like only he could do. Alongside him, Jimmy did his own version.

At Banning's table, Cheryl stopped the maitre d', the one Jimmy had offended with the five bucks. She handed him a hundred-dollar bill. This time he was satisfied. "Have the emperor stop by our table," Cheryl said to him.

"What are you doing?" Banning asked her grouchily.

"I'm showing an interest in the arts, like you always want me to," said Cheryl.

Onstage, James Brown and Jimmy were winding up for the big finale. "The way I like it is the way it is," they hollered together. "I got mine and don't worry 'bout his. Get on up and then shake your money maker, shake your money maker!"

"Hit me!" yelled James Brown.

"Hit you?" said Jimmy, not quite understanding this bit of showbiz slang.

The tuxedo arm snapped out and clocked James Brown. Again.

"*Whooo-aaah!*" James Brown yelled before hitting the deck.

The concert had been a great success. The audience fawned over Jimmy as he made his way, with Del, to Banning's table. He stopped to sign an autograph.

"Could you stop?" Del snapped at him. "I'd like to get to Banning's table before morning."

"I hate celebrities who brush off their fans," said Jimmy.

"Listen," Del told him. "Banning's girlfriend has been drinking. Her inhibitions will be lowered. She might reveal something to us that'll—Clark, will you stop waving!"

She lowered his hand. It was time for him to stop greeting his adoring fans. They approached Banning's table.

"We're honored," said Banning insincerely, "that you could join us." He turned to Rogers. "Go take care of that matter we discussed," he said. "Make some room."

Rogers got up and left.

Banning took a cigarette, and offered the pack to Jimmy. "Cigarette?" he asked.

"I quit," said Jimmy. "Bad for my voice."

Banning put the cigarette in his mouth. Instantly, the tuxedo arm snapped toward him, and a lighter slid into Jimmy's hand and lit the cigarette. "Thanks," said Banning.

Cheryl was utterly thrilled to have the Last Emperor of Soul right there beside her. "Singing is my favorite type of music," she gushed.

Banning made a halfhearted stab at introducing her. "Regrettably, my...Cheryl," he said.

As she leaned forward to shake hands, Jimmy could not help staring at a diamond brooch that resembled a winged spider, pinned to the shoulder of her tight-fitting white gown.

"Nice...to meet you," said Jimmy, still staring.

"You ever dance, unprofessionally?" she asked him coyly.

A moment later, they were walking to the dance floor. Jimmy tapped the watch for help.

"So," Jimmy said to her, trying to sound casual, "you and Diedrich seem very close. I bet he tells you everything."

Cheryl put her arms around him and they began to dance, only Jimmy was not quite moving to the rhythm that was being played. He tapped the watch, changing gears, until he hit the right dance.

"He tells me I move my hips too much when I dance," she said. "He's so critical. Where'd you learn to dance?"

"My mother sent me to tap-dancing lessons," he replied.

He twirled her, dipped her, and swung her around his hip. Cheryl giggled a bit too huskily and held him a bit too close.

Sitting at his table, Banning watched them dance. Del saw that she would need to distract him. She took a swallow of water, smacking her lips.

"Ninety-two Dasani," she said. "A gentle bouquet with a hint of vinyl polychloride. Earthy, yet ethereal." She held her glass up. "Cheers."

He looked at her, impressed, and clinked his glass against hers.

Out on the dance floor, Jimmy moved Cheryl gracefully. "What is Diedrich working on these days?" he asked her.

"Oh, a thingy. He told me about it but he uses all these big words and scientific mimbo-jimbo. You have a handsome face."

Jimmy was not sure how to respond. "So do you," he said.

"You're sweet," said Cheryl. "You know what I like about you? I can understand what you say."

"Really?" Jimmy did not realize that the reason for this was that she mangled the English language almost as much as he did.

"Yeah. Maybe we could go somewhere and talk." she suggested. "You seem like a great guy."

"Trust me," said Jimmy. "It's ninety percent the clothes."

They danced some more, and Jimmy suddenly jolted. "I think someone just pinched me," he said.

"I *know* someone did," said Cheryl. She winked lasciviously.

At the table, Del was flirting with Banning for all she was worth. "Crystal Geyser is sweet and fruity, a perfect complement to spicy foods and Asian cuisine, although it can leave a bitter aftertaste. But maybe my mouth is all wrong."

"Not at all," said Banning. "Your mouth is perfect."

"Show business is such a bore compared to water," Del said.

"It's my passion," Banning replied. "Some nights when I can't sleep I go down to my lab and play. I think of it as play rather than work."

"Maybe I can come play with you sometime. I'd love to see what you do," Del said.

He leaned close and touched her hand. "I want you to," he said, "but I have a problem... trusting people. Even those I know well."

"You're not unwise," said Del. "I'm not sure I trust myself with you, Diedrich."

"Let's think of a way you can prove yourself," he said.

Rogers appeared not far from the table and motioned to Banning. "Excuse me a moment," Banning said to Del. He got up and went over to Rogers.

Rogers spoke to Banning in a low voice. "Her name's Del Blaine. She's CSA," he said.

"I knew it was too good to be true," said Banning.

"And he's driving a car registered to Clark Devlin," Rogers informed him. "But we killed Devlin at Burger King."

"It appears he's back from the dead," said Banning. "And all over my date."

Banning grabbed Rogers's lapel. "Get Kells and Vic, and make sure you finish the job this time."

Rogers nodded and left.

Banning returned to the table just as Jimmy and Cheryl were returning from the dance floor. "I hope you'll excuse me," Banning said to the group. "Some urgent business just reared its ugly head." He turned to Cheryl. "Darling," he said, "would you mind if I left you and our newfound friends?"

He handed her a room key. "Here's the key to the hospitality suite," he said, "on the off chance you decide to spend the night in town."

Cheryl cast a lurid look at Jimmy. "If you have to go you have to go," she said to Banning gaily.

"Yes, I'm heartsick," he said. He turned and kissed Del's hand. "Until next time...goodnight."

He took his leave.

Cheryl did a big fake yawn that fooled nobody. "Well," she said, "since I'm staying in room 7268, I guess I'll just go up to room 7268 and take a nice hot bed and go to bath. In room 7268."

"Sounds yummy," said Del, sarcastically.

"Goodnight," said Jimmy.

Cheryl got up, bumped into another table, and headed off, swinging her hips.

"And once again we end up with nothing," Del said to Jimmy.

"I can get her to talk," he said.

"And say what?" She went into a brutal imitation of Cheryl: "Oh, Emperor, sign my bra!"

"I don't know what it is with you and bras,

but I think she has information," Jimmy said in his best agent voice.

"I see. That's why you're going to her hotel room."

"You've never seen me work. This is what Clark Devlin does best."

"Can I go home?" said Del disgustedly.

"No. You need to cover me."

"With what, a shot of penicillin? Fine, I'll be waiting by the pool. Can I at least have your jacket? It's cold." She got up to go.

"Sorry, I need my jacket," said Jimmy.

Now she was really disgusted. "You're quite the gentleman," she said. "I guess chivalry is dead."

A sexy woman walked by and put a cigarette in her mouth. The tuxedo reached out and lit it. The woman nodded and smiled at Jimmy—what a gentleman!

"Nice, really nice," said Del. "Thanks a lot." She stomped off.

The door to room 7268 was ajar. Jimmy entered the room, closed and locked the door. Immediately he saw Cheryl's purse, open on the table.

"Cheryl? Hello?" he called.

"Be right there," she replied from the bathroom.

Quickly but warily, Jimmy began digging through the contents of Cheryl's purse. The bathroom door opened and he jumped. Cheryl's fur coat flew out.

"Hang it for me, will you?" she called, sweetly.

Jimmy still had one hand deep in the purse. His other hand automatically snagged the coat. He reached toward the coat closet, balanced on one leg. The purse fell over, and Cheryl's compact, hairbrush and Palm Pilot spilled out.

Jimmy lunged and snatched up the things

before they hit the floor. He was still juggling them as he hung up Cheryl's fur.

At that moment, Cheryl stepped out of the bathroom.

Jimmy tossed the coat, which landed on the coat hook like a perfectly thrown horseshoe, and kicked the things he was juggling under the couch.

Cheryl was oblivious. "I know you can dance. What else can you do?" she asked.

"I'll show you," replied Jimmy, as he tapped the buttons on his watch.

━━◆◆━━

Outside by the pool, Del took the compact from her purse. She sat a moment, fighting with herself. Finally she gave in to her curiosity. "Okay, Devlin," she said to herself, "let's see your magic."

She opened the compact. On its tiny TV screen, she immediately saw Cheryl's ecstatic face.

"Oh, that's so good," Cheryl was moaning. "You're amazing."

"I should've stayed in the morgue," Del muttered.

Had she been able to take in the entire scene, she would have seen that Jimmy was giving Cheryl an energetic foot rub. "So," he was saying, "what about that good friend of Diedrich's—Walter Strider?"

"Ummm," Cheryl continued. "Never heard of him."

She took out a cigarette and put it between her lips. Jimmy was already on his way to the mirrored wet bar, but the suit had other ideas. He made a sharp detour, a lighter snapping into his hand, and lit her cigarette. Then he continued to the minibar.

"Who were those people at the table?" he asked her.

"They're Diedrich's closest associates," Cheryl said. "Very, very important."

"They're in the bottled-water business, too?" asked Jimmy.

"Is that what he does?" Cheryl asked. "I thought he made plastic doohickeys. Why don't you take off your jacket and stay awhile?" Cheryl said to Jimmy, pulling at his jacket.

"Okay," he said, as she pulled the jacket off of him. Jimmy's eyes fell on her pin. "Where did you get that pin?" he asked her.

"Diedrich. You know what I found out about this?"

He leaned in eagerly. "Tell me," he said, trying not to look too anxious.

She bent conspiratorially toward him. "They're not real diamonds," she whispered. "He's giving them away to everyone on the big release date."

Downstairs, Del watched, turning the TV to try to get a better angle on what was happening. She did not notice a shadow moving toward her among the stacked lounge chairs.

"And when is that?" Jimmy asked.

"Tomorrow night. You want to have a closer look?" she asked as she unpinned the pin and handed it to Jimmy.

He turned it over in his hands, studying it carefully.

"Will you excuse me, Emperor, while I go powder my nose?" she asked.

"Of course," said Jimmy, still looking at the pin.

In the corridor outside Cheryl's room, Kells and Vic were listening at the door. Vic expertly inserted some lock picks into the lock.

"Her voice reminds me of my mother," Kells snarled. Then he viciously kicked the in door.

Downstairs at the pool, Del saw Kells burst into the room. She sprang to her feet and ran toward the hotel doors, only to run smack into Rogers. He stepped out from behind the stacks of lounge chairs and clotheslined her, stiff-arming her across the throat.

Upstairs, Kells and Vic chased Jimmy around the room, but as he was wearing only the tux pants, he could only fight with his legs.

"I'll be right out!" Cheryl called.

"Take your time!" Jimmy panted. He sprang off a wall, using his head as a battering ram, nearly breaking his neck against Vic's chest but at least knocking the breath out of him.

Downstairs, Rogers dragged Del into the shadows. She kicked him in the head. They tumbled into the pool and tussled like sharks. But he was stronger than she was. He ended up standing and holding her head under the water.

Jimmy, meanwhile, had wrestled on the tux jacket. Now he was really cooking. He delivered a stunning series of punches and double kicks that sent Kells hurtling through a window and onto the balcony.

Jimmy followed him out to finish the fight. He looked down and saw Rogers holding Del underwater. He had to save her. Thinking fast, he kicked Kells over the balcony railing. Kells fell and fell, arms flapping wildly.

Del was looking up from underwater. She was running out of time. Bubbles bloomed from her mouth as Rogers shimmered above her.

Rogers was drowning her.

"Nice guys do finish la—" Rogers started to say. Then Kells hit him like a grand piano falling from the moon.

Upstairs, Jimmy was still double kicking

around the room, unable to stop the tuxedo. Vic was still down for the count.

Del appeared in the splintered doorway. Her soggy evening dress hung like moss. Her hair was plastered against her face. She watched Jimmy kick the air.

"This isn't what I signed up for!" yelled Del. "Enough! *Stop!*"

The tuxedo froze.

Jimmy turned to face her. "You scared it," he said.

"I'm not even going to ask," said Del.

Cheryl stepped out of the bathroom. "What have you been doing out here?" she said.

"Kicking back," said Jimmy.

Now Cheryl noticed Del. "Why is she here?" she demanded.

Del had had enough. She ran at Cheryl and head-butted her. Cheryl fell like a tree.

"Oh, that hurt!" said Del, rubbing her head. "But it was worth it."

It was time to go. Del and Jimmy came out of the room at about the same time that an old couple came out of theirs. They smiled fondly at Jimmy and Del as they passed.

"Honeymooners," said the woman to her husband.

14

In the kitchen of the Devlin mansion, Jimmy and Del cleaned each other's wounds with hydrogen peroxide, alcohol, and cotton balls.

Del winced. "Ouch! Can't you do anything?"

"Why are you so mad?" Jimmy asked her.

"Gee, let's think. Because big, ugly men are trying to kill me? Because I'm stuck with a millionaire playboy dilettante for a partner?"

"Whatever is in your head flies out your mouth," observed Jimmy. "You don't care how it makes people feel."

"I happen to be an extremely sensitive person," she retorted as she pushed an alcohol-soaked swab hard against a cut on Jimmy's forehead.

Now it was Jimmy's turn to wince. "You think you know feelings?" he said. "Look at me. How do I feel?"

He made a sad face.

"Sick," Del guessed.

"Sad!" he corrected her. "How about now?"

He made a worried face.

"Constipated," said Del.

"Worried," said Jimmy. No wonder you didn't get anything from Banning."

"Oh, right, I didn't get anything, except for where his lab is."

"Where?" said Jimmy.

Banning said sometimes he has trouble sleeping."

"All men have trouble sleeping," said Jimmy.

"Some nights he gets up and works in his lab," said Del.

"Oh. He sleeps in his lab?" asked Jimmy.

"The lab," explained Del as if to a child, "is at his house."

Jimmy realized this was the right answer. "Excellent!" he said. "You passed the test. I'll put in a good word with Chalmers."

"Let's go to CSA headquarters tonight. Chalmers will get a federal search warrant, give us enough backup to go out to Banning's and do a complete search—"

Jimmy shook his head. He thought fast. "I'm not sinking to the level of my superiors," he said.

"Keep Chalmers out of it. Just you and me, Del."

◗◖

At CSA headquarters, Steena sat and stared at a monitor. She was watching the surveillance tape recorded by the boutonniere camera.

In the tape, Cheryl moved toward "Devlin." The tuxedo was reflected in the mirror.

Devlin turned just before dropping out of the frame. Steena paused the tape, rewound it, and replayed it in slow motion. She punched a button, freezing the image.

She leaned close to the monitor screen. There was Jimmy—not Devlin—in the tux, a look of gleeful surprise on his face.

"*What!?*" shrieked Steena. "It's the limo driver!"

In five minutes, Chalmers was looking at the surveillance footage in his office. Randall, Joel, and Steena sat beside him, filled with anxiety.

"It doesn't appear Agent Blaine is in on this," said Steena. "We can pull her out, secure the tuxedo, remove Mr. Tong from play—"

"I have a feeling Banning will take care of that for us," said Chalmers, ominously.

"I wasn't talking about killing him," Steena pointed out.

"He's expendable," Chalmers replied, coldly.

15

It was a big night at the Banning estate. Cars and limos pulled up, letting the revelers off at the entrance to the huge house.

Del looked stunning in a long black gown. Jimmy, as usual, wore the tuxedo.

Del and Jimmy mixed with the throng. At the door, they spotted two Banning thugs collecting invitations.

"For a guy who wants to take over the world, he sure entertains a lot," Jimmy whispered to Del.

"Invitations?" asked one of the thugs officiously.

"Why don't you offer him five bucks?" Del snickered into Jimmy's ear.

Jimmy ignored her. "I have them somewhere," he said to the thug. He turned away and snatched an invitation from the pocket of a man nearby.

Slipping it inside his jacket, Jimmy pressed

some buttons on his watch. The green glow of a copying machine leaked from inside the jacket, and two perfectly duplicated invitations rose from his breast pocket. He handed them to the door thug.

"Thank you, Mr. Sanchez," said the goon.

Jimmy looked confused a moment, but then realized he was Mr. Sanchez. "*Gracias*," he said.

"Come, darling," he said to Del, escorting her in.

Banning's huge patio area was decorated for the big release of the new product. Guests danced around a reflecting pool as circus performers flew on cables and swooped over the crowd.

Jimmy and Del danced their way across the party area and onto the grounds. They wanted to get a look around.

They dropped back into shadows when they saw three Banning thugs carrying some sort of canisters.

"Let's follow them," Jimmy whispered.

"Why?" Del whispered back.

The thugs moved through an opening in a hedge.

"Why not?" said Jimmy. He pulled Del along.

"There's three of them," said Del.

"They'll lead us to the lab."

Jimmy and Del ducked through the hedge, following the men.

They now found themselves in a darkened area near a swimming pool. The diving board, strangely, was vibrating. The depth markings indicated that the pool was nine feet deep.

The thugs seemed to have disappeared.

"You have a way of saying things that are totally convincing and totally wrong," Del said to Jimmy.

"And you..." Jimmy made a yakkety-yak gesture with his hand. "Blah blah blah, talk too much, say too little."

He stood on the edge of the pool and stared into the depths.

"Don't tell me the great Clark Devlin can't come up with an answer," she mocked.

Jimmy stepped off the edge and walked across the surface of the water.

"Although you can walk on water," Del hastily added.

He moved to the middle, and Del stepped onto the diving board to have a better look.

"It's a trick, right?" she said.

The diving board tilted downward as the pool began, unbelievably, to split down the middle, the two halves moving apart. Jimmy straddled the split, looking down at a steep stairway. It was definitely a trick.

Jimmy and Del slid down a ramp alongside the flight of stairs. Hitting bottom, they found themselves in a corridor.

Del looked back up the ramp and the stairs. "Wheelchair accessible," she said. "At least Banning's an equal-opportunity sociopath."

They began to creep through the underground corridor, ready to face any attackers who might emerge.

Along the walls were display cases showcasing strange-looking insects.

"Devlin is very interested in insects," said Jimmy.

"What?" Del asked, confused.

Jimmy recovered fast. "Sometimes I speak of myself in the third person," he said. He pointed to himself. "Clark Devlin collects insects."

Del pointed to herself. "Del Blaine is getting annoyed."

Ahead they could see lights from an underground lab. They approached stealthily and sneaked into the large room.

In the lab was a grid of pools filled with nasty-looking liquids. Simms was talking to two lab-coated technicians near one of the pools. Del and Jimmy ducked down and listened.

"When you're done here," Simms said, "go sweep up the tunnel. And don't use the blower, I can tell the difference."

"Yes, Dr. Simms," said the technician.

"And don't drink the tequila," Simms added as the technician left. "It's for me and Mr. Banning."

He headed into another area of the lab.

"They don't pay us enough to put up with that overgrown geek," groused one of the remaining technicians.

"We better hope the little guys follow the queen or our stock options won't be worth squat," said another.

"Let's go have a smoke," said his companion.

Del and Jimmy waited for them to walk out. Once the coast was clear, they went into the lab. As Jimmy crossed the room to have a look at a map on the wall, Del walked over to examine the pools. She lifted her skirt and unstrapped a test kit from her thigh. It was right below her Beretta pistol.

Using a small pair of tongs, she dipped a test tube into the pool's foul liquid. Her test tube and the end of the tongs instantly dissolved. "I'm guessing this is toxic," she said, making a face.

"Look at this," Jimmy called her from the map. Del went over to look, examining the red lines that radiated from a central point.

Del gasped. "He's pinpointed the national reservoirs."

Jimmy looked at the vats, and then at the map. Horror flashed across his face. "He's going to poison the water," he said.

"Not with that stuff," she replied. "It's too detectable and there are government safeguards. Let's check the computer."

"Now you're thinking." Jimmy crossed the room to a large electronic device that was covered with dials and flashing lights.

"That's the stereo system," said Del. "Over here."

"You passed another test," said Jimmy.

She gave him a look, and they moved to the computer. He pulled out the chair for her. She sat down. Noticing a Post-it on the computer monitor, she ripped it off. "How sick is that?" she asked as she started typing.

"What?" asked Jimmy.

"They used 'Bambi' as a password."

Del started typing in commands, opening folders and files. The more she saw, the more alarmed she looked. "Oh my God," she whispered. "DNA recombinant microbes carrying a T4 genome."

"English," Jimmy prompted her.

"A genetically induced hydrogen-oxygen barrier—" she started.

"Normal person's English!" he exclaimed, interrupting Del in mid-sentence.

Del took a breath. "Dehydrating water. Drink it and you shrivel up and die," she explained. "Now the big question is, how can he possibly introduce it into the water supply?"

She glanced at Jimmy. He was making a face.

"Why are you smiling? Are you happy about this?" she said.

"No. This is my scared face. Look!" He pointed behind her: Three Banning thugs were coming at them from another section of the underground complex.

Del instantly shifted gears, pretending to be Jimmy's tipsy date. "*This* isn't a jacuzzi, you silly man!" she slurred.

Jimmy played along. "She's crazy for hot tubs," he told the goons. Then he slapped her on the rear as he ushered her toward the ladder. "Get going!" he said with a laugh.

The thugs grinned, and it seemed that Del and Jimmy had gotten away with their ruse. But then Simms appeared.

He watched them leave, his face clouded with suspicion.

Outside at the party, everyone was dancing. The music was great. Banning played the charming host, passing out diamond insect pins to the ladies. Around the perimeter of the party, Banning's thugs searched for the intruders.

Jimmy and Del danced together, hiding out in the crowd.

"Are you panicking?" Del asked him.

"Not so much."

"Me either," she agreed. "Banning's got the bacteria, but he still has to transport it from his lab to the water, and there's no way he can."

"Maybe with air," Jimmy mused.

"Not possible. Even if he could get to a reservoir undetected, alarms are triggered the second the surface of the water is broken."

"Really? I didn't know that," said Jimmy.

She looked at him. "You're doing it again, aren't you?"

"What?"

"You're always testing me, acting like you don't know when you do. You've taught me so much, not just about being an agent. I'm grateful to be the partner of the amazing and mysterious Clark Devlin," Del told him in a rare moment of sincerity.

He looked into her eyes and stopped dancing. "I want to tell you something," he said. "Clark Devlin is not who you think he is."

Del's cell phone rang. Quickly and quietly, she answered it. "Hello?" she whispered into the phone. "Steena, I can't talk now."

She listened.

As she listened, she resisted letting her face show the waves of emotion that were passing through her: disbelief, anger, hurt. "I understand," she said, calmly. "I can handle it."

She pressed END.

"Bad news?" Jimmy asked her.

"Can we try to find somewhere to be alone?" she said. She pulled him off the dance floor.

The closest place was a cabana bathroom. Del yanked Jimmy in and locked the door.

"I didn't know you were so strong," said Jimmy, amazed.

"Take off your clothes," she ordered him.

"Let's not do anything we'll regret—"

She raised her skirt, pulled the Beretta from its leg holster, and pointed it at his head. "I knew when I met you, you weren't Clark Devlin," she said. "You conned me. Now get that tuxedo off. It doesn't belong to you."

Jimmy sadly unbuttoned the tux. "I was going

to tell you," he said. "I'm Mr. Devlin's driver, he asked me to find Walter Strider—"

"I don't want to hear any more of your lies. Give me the watch. And the shoes. How did you think you'd get away with this?"

"Things happened. I decided to go with the flow."

"What about the underwear?" Del demanded.

"They're mine," said Jimmy, sheepishly.

Del left him in the cabana. Utterly distraught, her eyes brimming with tears, she made her way toward the exit with the tuxedo.

She was nearly clear, when her path was blocked by Rogers.

"It's impolite to leave without saying good-bye to the host," he sneered.

"I was just looking for Diedrich," she improvised.

"I'll take you to him," said Rogers. He put a huge hand around the back of her neck and maneuvered her through the dancers. "And this time," he added, "nothing's going to fall out of the sky and save you."

"You sure about that?" said Del.

Rogers couldn't stop himself from glancing up. Then he squeezed her neck a little harder.

Banning was waiting for them. He smiled as

he saw Rogers approach with Del in his big paw. "Like a big terrier with a little rat," he chuckled.

"I think she was down in the lab," Rogers told him.

"So at least," Banning said to Del, "your interest in water was genuine."

"Believe what you want," she said, "but I'm here because of you. You said you wanted proof that you could trust me. I bet this is just your size."

She held the tuxedo toward Banning.

The door to the cabana opened, and out sneaked Jimmy, clad only in boxers. He made his way to the driveway, where a number of limos were parked, waiting for their passengers.

Tiptoeing up behind a limo driver, Jimmy tried giving him a karate chop. The driver turned around, unfazed. He charged at Jimmy, who sidestepped him neatly. The driver's head hit the limo bumper, and he went out like a light.

Jimmy quickly stripped off the chauffeur's uniform. "I'll dry clean it and give it back," he promised the unconscious driver. Then he took the keys out of the pocket, got into the limousine, and drove away.

Jimmy drove through the night, wondering who the heck he was now.

After a while, he found himself back at Devlin's mansion. He sat alone wearing his favorite I-heart-NY T-shirt, composing a note of apology to Devlin and sipping from a bottle of water.

The desk was covered with papers and books. There were also several photographs of the bird-bath, the pictures Jimmy had noticed Devlin taking long ago.

"Dear Mr. Devlin," Jimmy wrote, "I did the best I could, but it was not good enough. I didn't find Walter Strider for you. I also lost your tuxedo. I'm sure you will get it back, and I will go back to being what I was before I met you—"

He reached for the water but because he wasn't looking, he knocked it over, spilling it across the photographs. Leaping up, he started to dab at the water with his shirttail. But then he stopped, noticing something.

The spill was magnifying a portion of one of the photographs. Something was there, on the surface of the water in the birdbath. It was an insect. He stared at the photo closely.

Right beside the photo was a book that was opened to a marked page. On the page was a clear photograph of an insect. Its skinny legs supported it above the water's surface, its feet resting on little cups of surface tension. His eyes went right to these words: *The water strider can literally walk on water, never breaking the thin layer of surface tension...*

Jimmy unfolded his hand. In it was Cheryl's rhinestone pin. He placed it on the page beside the picture. It was the same insect. And now he looked at the letter he was writing to Devlin. He looked at the name: "Walter Strider."

And then he put down the pen, so it covered the letter "l".

"Wa-ter Strider," he said to himself.

◣◗

The phone rang in Chalmers's office at the CSA. Randall answered it. "Mr. Chalmers," he said, "Jimmy Tong is on two."

"Who?" said Chalmers.

"Clark Devlin's driver," Randall reminded him. "He was calling for Del Blaine."

Chalmers picked up the phone. "Winton Chalmers," he said.

"I need to talk to Del Blaine," said Jimmy.

"Mr. Tong? Where are you?" Chalmers asked.

Jimmy ignored the question. "Is she there?"

"Miss Blaine is not your concern, nor mine at the moment," said Chalmers. "You have a piece of equipment belonging to us. It's in your best interests to return it."

"All you care about is that stupid tuxedo?" Jimmy yelled.

Chalmers paused. "Where are you, Jimmy?" he asked again.

Jimmy slammed the phone down, picked it up, and dialed again.

Kells answered: "Hello?"

"Is Del Blaine there?" Jimmy said.

"She's not free to talk," said Kells.

◄►

Chalmers was fit to be tied. "Did you get a trace?" he barked at Randall.

"It was too fast," Randall replied.

"Dammit," said Chalmers. "He could be working for Banning, for all we know. Find Del Blaine, now."

At that moment, Del was being led by Banning to a curtained area that contained some sort of hatchery. Rogers followed them, carrying Del's equipment: her gun, test kit, and the tuxedo.

Simms turned and looked up from his console. On the console was a silver tray on which stood a bottle of tequila, circled by six glasses. These were for the post-release celebration.

Simms looked disgruntled. "What is *she* doing here?" he demanded to know. "Diedrich?"

Banning took the tuxedo from Rogers and tossed it to Simms. "Analyze this," he said.

Del's cell phone rang. Rogers and Simms felt for their phones, before realizing that they had somehow neglected to take Del's phone from her.

"I thought you searched her," said Banning.

The phone kept ringing. Rogers followed the sound and tried to reach down the front of Del's dress, where she kept her phone. She slapped his hand.

"Excuse *me!*" she said.

She took out the phone and pressed a button on the underside, and a red light began to blink. Rogers snatched it from her and broke it in half.

"You couldn't take a message?" she said to him.

Across town sat an unmarked CSA van with a radio dish on the roof. In the van, the equipment started beeping. Two operatives sat at the control panel. On a locator screen, a red light began to blink. One of the operatives was talking on the phone. "We've got a positive location on Blaine, sir," he said.

"How long to get to her?" asked Chalmers's voice at the other end.

"Twenty minutes."

"Transmit the coordinates," Chalmers ordered. "We're on the move. Let's hope she can stall them."

◄►

In Devlin's mansion, Jimmy opened the closet in his room and grabbed his old knee-length coat. Then he stopped, noticing something. Hanging with all the uniforms was an opaque suit bag. Pinned to it was a note.

It read: "THE OTHER 10 PERCENT IS UP TO YOU. CLARK."

Jimmy unzipped the bag.

◥◣

In the hatchery, Banning held up a large glass pod with a beautiful green glow. "Miraculous nature," he said. "Look at my little darlings."

The globe was full of wriggling chrysalids, with winged insects emerging from them. "*Gerris maginatus*," Del said. "A species native to Southeast Asia, commonly known as the—"

Suddenly it dawned on her. "Walter Strider!" she gasped.

"Yes," beamed Banning, "the water strider. You do impress."

Simms appeared, holding the tuxedo. Hearing what he took for praise, he paused to listen.

"It's brilliant," Del said. "They touch down on reservoirs. Their little feet transfer deadly bacteria without breaking the surface, so no alarms sound, and it looks like another nasty trick of nature. Fortunately, there is one drinkable water source: yours."

Banning was thrilled. "Tah-dah. Banning Springs rules the world," he crowed.

Beside him, Simms smiled proudly.

"Dietrich, you're a genius," said Del. "Too bad it won't work."

Simms's smile flickered off. He stepped forward. "It will so!" he whined. "My plan is perfect!" He caught Banning's look. "I mean your and my plan...our plan."

"Hush up, Simms," barked Banning. He turned to Del. "Explain," he said.

"All righty," she said, glancing at her watch and figuring out a way to stall for time. "The life cycle of *Gerris maginatus* begins with mating. The insects swarm to fresh water, where the fertilized eggs are deposited on the underside of lotus leaves and hatch into larvae, which enter a rather lengthy pupa stage—"

"Spare me the Discovery Channel blather," said Banning. "Just tell me why it won't work."

"Yes, tell us," said Simms, sounding like a nasty little boy.

"Why won't it work?" Del vamped as mind scrambled for a convincing explanation. "Because ...because this is the northern hemisphere. Correct? You've incubated insects native to the southern hemisphere. So, it's simply too cold for them to mature sexually—much like Simms here. Therefore, they won't mate and therefore, they won't seek out water," she concluded in triumph.

Banning leveled his gaze at Simms, who was blinking rapidly. "Is this true?" Banning said.

"Diedrich, you're not going to believe this little woman!" protested Simms.

"Oh yeah?" said Del. "Ask him if I lied about the tuxedo."

"Simms?" said Banning.

"It's...good," Simms allowed.

"Good?" Del shouted. "It's the most incredible piece of technology on the planet, and I laid it in your big hot hands."

"Diedrich, I beg you, release the bugs," Simms pleaded.

Del took the jacket from Simms's trembling hands and held it up. "Go ahead and do what he tells you," she taunted Banning. "You might win second prize at a junior-high-school science fair, but forget your dreams of world domination."

Banning looked at her, trying to decide whether he trusted her.

"Slip into it, Diedrich," Del continued. "See how it feels."

Banning slipped his arms into the jacket, and it instantly molded to his body. Pleased, he smiled at Del.

Meanwhile Jimmy, wearing his old knee-length coat, was outside Banning's estate. Once again, he approached the officious thug at the door.

"Sanchez, right?" said the thug, pleased with himself.

"Wrong," said Jimmy. He grabbed the man's tie and pulled him close. "Go tell your boss Clark Devlin is back," he said.

There was the sound of pistols being cocked, and suddenly Jimmy's head was surrounded by four gun barrels.

Downstairs in the hatchery, Banning was now completely attired in the tuxedo.

"It drapes nicely," he admired.

Banning scrolled the watch. Then he took a couple of warmup strides and went into a few flips, demonstrating his prowess with the tuxedo. "And it does put a spring in one's step," he added. He looked tickled pink.

"Happy to have lightened your loafers," said Del.

"One question," said Banning. "Why are you doing this?"

"Besides the unspeakably huge sums you'll pay me to fiddle with your bugs?" she replied, surreptitiously checking her watch again. "I'm sick of working for pompous bureaucrats and incompetent dilettantes where the only challenge is trying not to laugh in their faces."

"Are you always so long-winded?" Banning asked her.

The estate's alarms sounded loudly.

"Only when I have to be." Del smiled.

"What's this?" said Banning tensely.

"I believe it's the moment," said Del, "When fifty CSA commandos storm in and take you, your pretentious accent, your stupid sideburns, and your friend off to the federal pen. Where, by the way, they serve nothing but heavily chlorinated tap water."

The corridor outside the hatchery was now filled with shadows and the sound of footsteps.

Banning grabbed Del, ready to use her as a hostage.

But there was no need. The people who emerged from the shadows were Kells and Vic, hauling Jimmy.

Del continued as if nothing had ever happened. "So," she said, "do I have the job or not?"

"Dr. Simms," ordered Banning, "prepare for release!"

Simms sneered at Del. "With pleasure!" he said.

Glowing with excitement, Simms hit a sequence of buttons on the console.

"I could have forgiven all but the stupid sideburns remark," Banning said to Del.

Slowly, the curtains parted, revealing the vaulted ceiling of the hatchery. It was hung with teardrop shaped pods that glowed and pulsated. It was beautiful, magical even.

"Release protocol initiated," said the female computer voice.

The console lights blinked and beeped.

Del moved to Jimmy. "Why are you here?" she whispered.

"I'm saving you," he said weakly.

"That's very nice, but where are the big men with the big guns?" she whispered.

Jimmy shrugged.

"Maturation level seventy-five percent," said the computer.

Banning pushed Del aside, reached down, and pulled Jimmy close. "For years I've heard about you," he said. "The legendary Casanova, the worldly wit, the invincible super-agent. And now that we meet I find that the great Clark Devlin is nothing more than an ordinary man, about to die an extraordinary death."

"You're right. Except for one thing. The name is Tong. Jimmy Tong."

And with those words, Jimmy leaped to his feet and tore off his overcoat, revealing a super-cool high-tech suit.

Kells and Vic immediately came at him but,

using the coat as a weapon, he took them both out at once.

"Let's not get too cocky," Banning warned. He launched his tuxedo-clad body at Jimmy, and the fight was on. Jimmy fought hard, holding his own, but his suit was clearly not as powerful as Banning's tuxedo.

"Maturation level one hundred percent," announced the computer's voice.

"Simms! Open the hatch!" Banning ordered.

Simms reached for a lever on the control console, but Del ran to stop Simms from opening the hatch.

Rogers tried to block her. She head-butted him and he fell into a pool and began to sizzle. Good-bye, Rogers.

Del grabbed a beaker filled with mutant water and flung it onto the console. Simms jerked his hands away from the controls, which had begun to sizzle and melt. A sign lit up: HATCH MALFUNCTION!

"Diedrich, she's ruining everything!" wailed Simms.

Banning looked up at the closed hatch and spotted a manual release. He kicked Jimmy, knocking him to the edge of a pool, where he teetered on the edge.

Banning ran to the hatchery, but Jimmy

amazingly recovered his balance and raced after Banning.

As Del watched Jimmy chase Banning, Simms tried to fix his ruined console. Failing, he turned petulantly to Del.

"I knew mean girls like you in high school!" he said.

"Did they do *this*?" asked Del, kneeing him in the groin.

"Yes, they did," he groaned as he crumpled to the floor.

"You take away your high-tech stuff and you're nothing but a big, whiny nerd," she taunted him.

He grabbed the bottle of tequila, took a swig to dull the coming pain, and then smashed his hand through a glass fireax case.

"With a very big ax," said Del, a touch of apprehension in her voice.

Simms, in a total rage, took a swing at her. She dodged the ax, but it snagged and ripped her dress, tearing it into a miniskirt.

"This is Armani and I paid for it myself!" she shouted.

Across the lab, Banning scrolled his watch and leaped fifty feet straight up to the hatch's manual release.

Jimmy scrolled *his* watch and leaped, but

rose only ten feet or so. "Ah, lousy suit!" he said in exasperation when he landed.

There was nothing for Jimmy to do but climb, using his own strength to reach Banning.

Simms, meanwhile, was chasing Del into the hatchery, swinging at her with the ax.

"Devlin! I mean, Jimmy! Help!" Del yelled.

"I'm busy!" panted Jimmy.

Up near the ceiling, Banning was turning a huge wheel that opened the hatch. Jimmy clambered to the top in time to grapple with Banning, trying to close the hatch again.

Jimmy looked down and saw that Del was in trouble. He kicked one of the pods free, sending it plummeting toward Simms.

Using Jimmy's brief moment of inattention, Banning spoke softly into the watch. "Strangle!" he instructed.

Down on the floor, Simms saw the pod heading toward him, and dropped the ax. It bounced into the moat and dissolved in a smoky sizzle. The pod then hit him, giving Del the chance to attack. She pummeled his face.

"Face, stomach, face, stomach," she recited from her manual.

Simms reeled away from her and fled, which allowed Del to notice that Jimmy was now in trouble. The pods were opening, and the water striders were flying out in great swarms. Banning, meanwhile, had his hands grasped firmly around Jimmy's throat.

Jimmy seemed to have no defense against Banning, who was literally squeezing the life out of him. Jimmy slugged Banning in the face, with no effect. He hit him again with all his might. Banning only grinned. The tuxedo was all-powerful.

Thinking fast, Del took hold of a hose that was dangling nearby and whipped it upward, entangling Banning's feet. She pulled, trying to dislodge him. But her efforts only caused Jimmy to suffer more strangulation. Banning kicked his legs, and the power of the tuxedo sent Del flying. She ended up dangling above the acid moat.

With the last of his strength, Jimmy reached out his hand and dipped his fingers into Banning's pocket. He pulled out a cigarette and put it between his own lips.

"Don't you know that's hazardous to your health?" Banning taunted him.

"No, to yours," said Jimmy.

The tuxedo's arm flew off Jimmy's throat; it just had to light the cigarette. Jimmy shoved the flaming lighter into Banning's smirking face and knocked him out.

Banning plunged downward, landing face-first on the metal bridge, which was damp with water from the acid moat. His face instantly simmered.

Jimmy looked at the cigarette with disgust and threw it down. "I quit," he declared.

Then he noticed Del, still dangling from the hose. Her feet were about to go into the acid.

Jimmy swung to the floor, leaned out at an impossible angle, and snagged Del, just before she went into the acid.

"You're alright?" he asked her.

"Nice going. Now millions of people are going to die from dehydration." Del pointed up. "You left the hatch open."

"Because I had to save you!" Jimmy protested.

"Oh, you're going to blame me for this disaster?"

Jimmy looked up at the circling cloud of insects. "They're not flying away," he observed.

"Yeah," she agreed. "What are they waiting for?"

Jimmy suddenly had a flash of insight. "They are waiting...to follow the queen!" he said.

"I was just going to say that!" said Del, annoyed. "They're *Gerris maginatus*! Asian water striders follow their queen."

Jimmy walked to the fountain, reached in,

and pulled out a crystal globe about the size of a volleyball. He held the glowing orb toward Del.

"As long as we have her," Del said, "the water striders aren't going anywhere."

"Let's roll," said Jimmy.

Holding the orb in his hands, Jimmy took off running toward the exit. Del was right behind him.

Suddenly Simms and about twenty of Banning's goons appeared in the opening from the corridor. Jimmy, seeing the passage blocked, stopped dead in his tracks. Del slammed into him. The glass globe with the queen soared through the air and shattered.

"I've saved the queen!" Simms crowed.

The queen fluttered up and out. Everyone stopped moving. All eyes followed the luminous insect as she flew up and up.

Del turned her face upward, like everyone else. Then the queen fluttered down—and landed on Del's nose.

Del stared cross-eyed at the insect, which seemed to be looking at her.

"Don't move!" Jimmy commanded.

Nobody moved.

Jimmy cocked his arm as if he was going to swat the insect. "No!" cried Del.

Okay, he'd have to try something else. He

grabbed a tequila shotglass from the silver tray and placed it over Del's nose, trapping the queen.

The buzzing of the cloud of hovering water striders intensified.

"What are you waiting for?" Simms demanded. "Get her!"

Now the thugs rushed Jimmy and Del. As he fought off the attackers, Jimmy was also trying to contain the trapped queen. He moved the shotglass to Del's chest, to her shoulder, to her back.

Simms rushed at Del. She kicked him, and he prudently decided to take refuge under the console.

The tide of the fight began to turn. Jimmy and Del dispatched attacker after attacker until the last few fled.

Slowly, carefully, Jimmy moved the trapped queen to his palm.

"It's hard to believe," said Del, "but I think we finally aced a mission."

Behind Del's back, Banning rose up. Half his face was scarred by the grid pattern of the metal bridge.

Jimmy saw him over Del's shoulder.

"That doesn't look like your happy face," Del said quizzically, noticing Jimmy's horrified expression.

Banning hurtled toward Jimmy, his mouth wide open in a deafening scream.

Del was in the way, and there was no time for Jimmy to explain the problem. There was nothing for him to do but kick her feet out from under her, clearing the way.

"Come and get it!" Jimmy challenged Banning.

Jimmy released the queen. Then he caught her again in the glass and hurled the glass—with the queen—right into Banning's open mouth.

Banning swallowed.

The hovering swarm of insects descended like a funnel cloud, straight toward Banning's mouth.

Del got to her feet, realizing what Jimmy had done. Banning fell backward. His skin swiftly wrinkled up and turned to parchment.

Jimmy shielded Del's eyes, but she knocked his hand away. "Excuse me, I deserve to see this!" she said.

In seconds, Banning's body had dissolved to dust, leaving the tuxedo nicely laid out on the floor.

Now they heard the sound of men running. Jimmy turned to face more attackers, but Del stopped him. "Don't worry, Jimmy," she said. "They're CSA."

The CSA commandos, in their black suits, rushed into the lab, guns and badges drawn.

Joel ran up to Jimmy and punched him, dropping him to the floor. "Are you okay?" he asked Del.

"Nice work, Joel," she replied. "You just decked the hero."

Jimmy got to his feet as more CSA agents stormed in.

Randall pulled Simms out from under the console. "Thank God you're here!" Simms gibbered at him. "I tried to stop him myself, but I'm just a lowly employee—"

"He's the evil genius," Del explained.

As Randall slapped handcuffs on him, Simms could not help but smile at this recognition. "Okay, okay. I'll testify for a little immunity," he offered, though nobody had asked.

After Simms was taken away, Chalmers swaggered up to Jimmy and Del. "Looks like we got here just in time," he said.

"To what? Take credit?" Del said acidly.

"You're hilarious, Blaine," said Chalmers. He turned to Jimmy. "Winton Chalmers, director, CSA," he introduced himself. "I spearheaded the operation that took down Diedrich Banning. I'll bet you're Jimmy Tong."

"Good guess," said Jimmy. He pointed to the floor. "There's your tuxedo," he said. "Hope you're happy."

"I will be once I get it safely back to headquarters," said Chalmers. "By the way, Blaine, not a bad job for your first time in the field."

"I didn't do it alone," she said.

"She's always saying nice things about me," Jimmy said with a wry grin.

"When you do something right for a change you deserve credit," she said.

"I'm honored just to know I helped the United States of America," said Jimmy.

"That's how I feel, too, soldier," said Chalmers.

Del wheeled on Chalmers. "You think you can get away with a perfunctory pat on the head, you cowardly bureaucratic weasel? Sir?"

"Hoping to," replied Chalmers with perfect equanimity.

"Maybe there is one thing you could do for me," said Jimmy.

17

Two vans blocked the intersection leading to the city plaza. They were outfitted for every possible type of surveillance. Inside the first van, Steena sat before a complex panel of instruments.

"We're at T-minus-thirty and counting," said Steena in a low voice. "Is everyone in position?"

Several voices answered affirmatively.

"Okay," Steena said, "we're good to go."

On a roof overlooking the plaza, the real Clark Devlin hunkered over some high-tech listening equipment. "This has got to slide like butter," he said.

"If we don't deliver the package, we can kiss democracy good-bye," he said. "What's his current condition?"

In the second van, Del Blaine was sitting with Jimmy and talking on a headset. "He's relaxed," she reported.

"I'm not relaxed," said Jimmy.

"He's gonna be fine," Del said. "It's new territory, but he's ready."

She turned to Jimmy. "Are you ready?" she asked him.

"I forgot what to say."

"You can do this. Just focus," she ordered

Steena's voice came over the intercom. "We're gonna miss it if we don't move now," she said.

"Go! Jimmy Tong!" Del yelled, opening the van's cargo door and pushing him out.

Launched out of the van, Jimmy moved down the street, his vision darting. His breathing was speeding up. Sweat beaded on his lip. He was trying hard to keep himself together. He pressed the earpiece to his ear.

Del's voice came through it. "You hear me?" she said.

"Yes," Jimmy replied.

"Good luck."

His hand reached out. He pushed through the glass doors.

And he was in the art gallery.

His breath was heavy; his heart pounded. He looked around, searching.

"He's freezing up," said Devlin's voice.

Del's voice replied. "He's okay. Everybody stay calm."

Then Jimmy saw her. The beautiful, unattainable Jennifer.

"He's locked on target," said Del's voice.

Jimmy's face was tight with concentration. He headed toward her. It seemed as if time itself had slowed down.

Peter Strick, the gallery owner, appeared. He was heading over to cut Jimmy off.

"Hostile force closing!" said Steena's voice urgently. "Take him out!"

Instantly, Randall and Joel turned from pretending to look at a painting. They grabbed Strick and touched a metal wand to his forehead, causing him to go limp. Without further ado, they dragged him behind a sculpture.

"Nicely done," Steena's voice congratulated them.

Jimmy continued moving toward Jennifer. He reached her. His lips began to move, but no words came out.

"Yes?" said Jennifer.

He was stuck. He grinned at her, trying to think of what to say.

"Tell her her skin looks radiant," Devlin's voice said into his ear.

"Or hopefully something slightly less hokey," disagreed Del's voice. "It doesn't have to be brilliant. Start with hello."

"Uh..." Jimmy began.

"Is there something I can show you?" Jennifer inquired.

"Come on! Your posture's slumping!" said Del's voice in his ear. "Straighten up and talk!"

"I can't think with you screeching in my ear!" Jimmy yelled, totally flustered.

Jennifer backed up.

"Not you! Her!" Jimmy explained to Jennifer, pointing to his head.

"I'm sorry, but you'll have to leave," said Jennifer. She looked alarmed.

"Way to go," said Del's voice. "Now she thinks you're psycho."

"I'm not psycho!" Jimmy yelled.

Now Jennifer ducked behind a desk and came up holding a can of mace. "Get out!" she screamed.

"Terminating mission!" said Steena's voice through the earphone. "Pack it up and roll on home."

Jimmy yanked the earplug out of his ear and stalked out of the gallery.

When he reached the van, Del leaped out. "At least you're consistent," she said to him. "You totally blew that."

"It's difficult for me," said Jimmy.

"What's so hard? You just say something like, 'Excuse me, want to go get a cup of coffee?'"

"When I get around a beautiful woman I can't talk," he said.

"Oh, thank you very much," said Del.

"What's the matter?" he asked her.

"Nothing."

"What?"

"You can't tell how I feel?" she asked, making a face.

"You look sad," Jimmy said.

"No—"

"Sick?" he asked.

"No—"

"Constipated?" he continued.

"No! Nothing!" Del yelled.

"Wait!" said Jimmy. "I know! You have a crush on me."

"How do you say 'delusional' in Chinese?" she replied.

"Tell me what's wrong," said Jimmy.

Del took a breath, gathering her courage to admit what she felt. "I guess what it is, is...no guy would ever do something for me like what you did...tried to do."

"I can explain why," he said. "Because you're a pain in the butt."

"Yeah, well, thanks. Nice workin' with you, too." She turned and started walking towards the second van.

The van pulled away. She sighed and kept walking.

Jimmy watched her walk away. She walked; he watched.

"Excuse me," he finally said. "Want to go get a cup of coffee? I'll give you some 'guy' tips."

She stopped. She turned. "I only drink organic green tea," she said.

Jimmy shook his head. She was being a pain in the butt again.

"Alright, fine, coffee," she said. "I love coffee."

He offered his arm and she took it.

"No more blah, blah, blah, blah, blah," he said. "And I'll let you pay."

They walked off toward some distant café.